"Hey, someone ⎯⎯⎯⎯⎯⎯⎯⎯⎯," Bob said, as if it were a truly astonishing phenomenon. "How about that?"

"Pretty weird," I agreed. I casually glanced toward the take-out counter to see who was getting my favorite pie.

A guy was standing there. But not just any guy. My jaw dropped when I saw him. He was gorgeous.

He looked about my age and had the kind of naturally curly hair that always looks a little unruly, even when it's clean and short, as his was. The kind of hair a girl just wants to run her hands through. It didn't hurt one bit that he was also tall, handsome, and built like an athlete. When he turned his head to scan the room, I averted my eyes so he wouldn't notice me staring at him. But I did notice an adorable cleft in his chin. I also thought I'd detected a hint of a fascinating intensity in his eyes. Maybe I was just making up that last part out of sheer boredom and desperation. But suddenly I knew that this guy was someone I absolutely had to meet.

He's the One

Nina Alexander

BANTAM BOOKS
NEW YORK • TORONTO • LONDON • SYDNEY • AUCKLAND

RL 6, age 12 and up

HE'S THE ONE

A Bantam Book / June 1998

Produced by Daniel Weiss Associates, Inc.
33 West 17th Street
New York, NY 10011.
Cover photography by Michael Segal.

ISBN: 0-553-49250-0

Published simultaneously in the United States and Canada

Bantam Books are published by Bantam Books, a division of Bantam
Doubleday Dell Publishing Group, Inc. Its trademark, consisting of the
words "Bantam Books" and the portrayal of a rooster, is Registered in
U.S. Patent and Trademark Office and in other countries. Marca
Registrada. Bantam Books, 1540 Broadway, New York, New York 10036.

PRINTED IN THE UNITED STATES OF AMERICA

OPM   0 9 8 7 6 5 4 3 2 1

One

Jill

THE DATE WASN'T going well.

I knew it from the moment we sat down at my favorite pizza hangout. Well, actually, that's not exactly true. I *suspected* it from the moment we arrived at Niko's Boardwalk Pizzeria. I *knew* it from the moment Bob started to describe the scavenging habits of a seashell-type critter called the common northern whelk in great detail. You think I'm kidding? Think again.

I concentrated on my food as Bob droned on. By the time I'd finished my first slice he'd moved on to even duller topics—something to do with the chambered nautilus. Or maybe it was the two-spotted keyhole limpet. I nodded now and then and concentrated on my pizza: the spicy sauce special with extra capers.

Suddenly Bob interrupted his description of the carnivorous brown-banded wentletrap to lean across the small Formica-topped table and gaze into my eyes. "You've been awfully quiet, Jill," he said. "Why don't you tell me more about yourself?"

"There's not much more to tell," I told him.

Bob's eyes widened in surprise. "I find that hard to believe."

I stared back at him and thought about what a shame it was—Bob really was cute. That's why I hadn't picked up on his inner nerdiness right away. His big blue eyes had suckered me in the moment I'd met him. Still, I never should've made a date with someone I'd just met. Usually I liked to keep things more casual with a brand-new guy—especially a transient. My friend Donna came up with that term, *transient*. Transients are the people who come to spend a week, a month, or the entire summer at Lenape Beach, our little hometown on the Delaware shore. Then they return to Washington or Philadelphia or Baltimore or wherever they live, and Lenape Beach transforms back into a quiet town until the next summer.

For some reason I'd thrown caution to the wind with Bob. I don't know, maybe it was his hunky, muscular shoulders, a result of his years on the wrestling team. That's what he'd talked about when we'd met during a beach volleyball game a couple of days earlier—wrestling. I'd pegged him as a jock, which was fine with me. I like sports. I've hung out with lots of sports-crazy guys, and they're usually really fun.

But Bob wasn't fun. And he wasn't a sports nut.

Just a nut. Forget the Phillies or the Redskins. Bob was a fan of the frilled dogwinkle and the measled cowrie. And now this nut was waiting to hear all about me. Since I wasn't a chambered nautilus or even a lowly scallop, I doubted my life story would interest him much, even if I did feel like sharing it. Which I didn't. Maybe I was impulsive, but I wasn't stupid. I never got in too deep with any of the guys I hung out with. And I wasn't going to start with this one.

"Really," I insisted. "There's not much to tell. I live in Lenape Beach year-round, go to school at Lenape High—basically boring stuff."

"Come on," Bob said with a grin. "You must have good stories about growing up at the beach. Growing up gorgeous. Stuff like that."

"Thanks for the compliment. But no, not really." I've learned not to take flattery too seriously. I've heard all the lines: that my long blond hair looks like spun gold, that my greenish blue eyes sparkle like the sea on a summer's day, that I look awesome in a bikini—okay, so not all guys are poets. But just because some guy compliments you doesn't mean that you should spill your guts to him.

"Okay." Bob picked up a piece of his sausage pizza. "Then can I ask you a few questions about some of the beaches?"

"Sure," I said absently.

I glanced at the door as Bob started to ask me something about the tidal conditions at the local beach. According to the big clock on the wall over

Niko's take-out counter, the gastropod guy and I had been sitting there for almost an hour. That meant Annabelle should be arriving any minute.

When you went out as much as I did, you came up with lots of little checks and balances to keep things running smoothly. And that night my friend Annabelle was playing the role of Ms. Checks and Balances. She, Donna, and our other best friend, Tim, took turns whenever I needed them. Date duty, they called it. Donna and Tim were out celebrating their five-month anniversary, so Annabelle had promised to drop by Niko's on her way to her play rehearsal in case things weren't working out.

Come on, Annabelle, I thought. *Where are you?*

At that second the door swung open and Annabelle strode in. She never misses a cue.

Annabelle's an actress, and she looks like one too. At five foot six I'm not exactly short, but Annabelle towers over me by a good four inches. And somehow the way she carries herself makes her look even taller. Annabelle's hair also adds a few inches—it's flaming red and springs out all over her head in soft, perfect ringlets that fall halfway down her back.

Annabelle paused just inside the door to nod hello to Niko, then looked over at my table. I reached up with both hands and casually ran them through my hair. It was a simple signal but an effective one. Guys never suspected a thing.

Annabelle smirked at me, then swung into her

role. Her hazel eyes grew wide and frightened; her face got pale and pinched. She rushed toward us.

"Jill!" Annabelle exclaimed loudly. "I'm so glad I found you!"

"Oh, hello, Annabelle." I pretended to be surprised. "Bob, this is a good friend of mine, Annabelle Taylor."

"Hi." Bob twisted around in his chair to give Annabelle a polite smile. As he turned, the massive muscles in his broad, square shoulders rippled a little. For a second I almost changed my mind.

Then I remembered the chambered nautilus. "What's up?" I asked. "You don't look so good."

Annabelle grasped my arm. "I know. I've got my very first play rehearsal tonight, and I don't know if I can do it. I'm terrified. You've got to help me!"

"Annabelle is playing Eliza Doolittle in *My Fair Lady* at the dinner theater here in town," I explained to Bob. That was all true enough. But the show had been rehearsing for weeks. And Annabelle has never had a moment of stage fright in her life. She'd played Annie at the same theater when she was six, and one of the daughters in *Fiddler on the Roof* a year later. She was more at home onstage than off.

"You've got to help me, Jill," Annabelle begged again. She was good. If I hadn't known better, *I* would have believed her act. "I'm really sorry to interrupt and everything, but you've got to come to rehearsal with me. Please? I need moral support."

I pretended to struggle with her request for a

5

moment. I wasn't a professional like Annabelle, but I wasn't a bad actress myself. It was a skill I'd picked up during my parents' divorce, and it had served me rather well since I'd started dating. "Well . . . ," I said, trying to sound reluctant.

"I think it's a great idea, Jill," Bob stated.

"What?" I stared at him. This was an unexpected twist. Was Bob actually looking for an excuse to ditch *me?*

Bob smiled and pushed back his chair. "Your friend needs moral support," he said, standing up. "And we're almost finished eating, right? Watching a play rehearsal sounds like fun. We can both go cheer her on."

Annabelle's eyes widened again, this time in dismay. "Um, that's okay," she said quickly. "I just remembered. Mr. Dinsdale doesn't like anyone to come to rehearsals who isn't in the cast."

That was a bigger lie than all the rest. Mr. Dinsdale was a local legend. He'd been directing the plays at the Lagoon Dinner Theater for almost twenty years, and he was totally easygoing. Also completely loony. He loved it when people came to watch his rehearsals—as long as those people were locals. He had several of his own descriptive names for the summer visitors, none very flattering. The only time he liked to see transients was when they were sitting in the audience for one of his shows.

I'd known Mr. Dinsdale forever. He was good friends with my father. Despite that, I still thought he was pretty cool. Lately I mostly saw Mr.

Dinsdale at Annabelle's rehearsals, which Donna and Tim and I attended faithfully whenever we could. Annabelle really did appreciate our moral support, stage fright or no stage fright.

Bob looked disappointed. "Are you sure?" he asked. "I mean, I don't know much about music or plays or anything. But it would be kind of cool to see a rehearsal."

"Sorry." Annabelle dropped my arm. She had also dropped the act, although Bob probably didn't realize it, since she still looked nervous. "Um, I'd better get going," she added with a weak smile. "Just talking to Jill has made me feel a lot better already. See you." She turned and raced for the door.

"Bye," Bob called after her. He turned back to me. "Too bad. That could've been fun." He reached over and squeezed my shoulder. "Maybe we can go see the show together sometime."

"Um, maybe." I tried to return his smile. "But actually, I think opening night isn't until August. After you go back home."

That was another lie. The first performance was less than two weeks away. I hoped Bob didn't hear about it.

"Oh, well." Bob didn't seem terribly upset. He picked up another slice of pizza. "Now, what were we talking about?"

Bob forgot about the beach questions he'd started to ask me. Instead, he returned to his enthusiastic monologue about the secret life of seashells. I stuffed pizza into my mouth and tried to come up with an alternative plan. Bob clearly wasn't the type to take a hint. That meant it wouldn't be easy to get rid of him even after we finished eating.

Maybe Donna and Tim will wander in and rescue me, I thought hopefully. But I knew it wasn't going to happen. Donna and Tim had reservations at the Ocean Pearl, the fanciest restaurant in town. After filling their stomachs with fantastic seafood, the chances were slim that they would decide to stop by Niko's for a snack. Instead, they would probably take a romantic stroll along the beach. Even though I was trying hard to accept the fact that two of my best friends were now a couple, my mind continued to balk at that image.

Bob was still talking. He didn't seem to notice that I wasn't listening anymore. I'd gone out with guys like that before—guys who took over the conversation and never let it go. Granted, most of them weren't obsessed with seashells. That was new. But I knew what I had to do.

There was just one question. How was I going to do it without my friends' help?

I counted on my friends in situations like this. That was partly because the four of us—Annabelle, Donna, Tim, and I—count on each other for all sorts of things. We always have. We've been inseparable since kindergarten.

But mostly it's because I really hate confrontation.

Donna was the first to point that out. She wants to study psychology when she gets to college, so she's always psychoanalyzing everybody she knows.

I'm one of her favorite subjects. She says I avoid confrontation because of my parents' divorce, which happened when I was ten. It wasn't a nasty breakup, or a scary one, or a bitter one. I guess it was what they call "amicable." One day my mother casually mentioned to my brother and me that Dad would be moving out the next day. That was about it. He lived across town for a month or two, then moved up to Dover to live with the ex-wife of an air force mechanic. Meanwhile, my mother put on a brave face and refused to talk about it. However, she did insist on sending my brother and me to weekly appointments with the school psychologist, a total idiot who seemed to think that everything we said or did called for endless analysis and discussion.

The upshot of all that family history is that I didn't know how to get rid of Bob without being totally blunt and rude—in other words, honest. Donna would have said that my problem with being honest was due to lessons I'd learned in childhood.

I suppose she would have been right. In any case, I didn't want to hurt Bob's feelings. He might not have been for me, but he wasn't exactly the devil either. He was just a perfectly nice guy who happened to be duller than dirt. Or maybe I should say duller than a dolphin-toothed nut clam.

Just then came one of those moments of absolute quiet. It was as if everyone in the place chose that precise time to take a sip of soda or a bite of pizza. Niko's voice rang out clearly through the room.

"Yo, Julio! Get me that spicy sauce special," he yelled to his assistant. "Heavy on the capers!"

"Hey, someone ordered the same pizza as you," Bob said, as if it were a truly astonishing phenomenon. "How about that?"

"Pretty weird," I agreed. I casually glanced toward the take-out counter to see who was getting my favorite pie.

A guy was standing there. But not just any guy. My jaw dropped when I saw him. He was gorgeous.

He looked about my age and had the kind of naturally curly hair that always looks a little unruly, even when it's clean and short, as his was. The kind of hair a girl just wants to run her hands through. It didn't hurt one bit that he was also tall, handsome, and built like an athlete. When he turned his head to scan the room, I averted my eyes so he wouldn't notice me staring at him. But I did notice an adorable cleft in his chin. I also thought I'd detected a hint of a fascinating intensity in his eyes. Maybe I was just making up that last part out of sheer boredom and desperation. But suddenly I knew that this guy was someone I absolutely had to meet.

Bob was talking about the plight of the lugubrious thorn drupe.

I couldn't stand it anymore. I had to take action. And I had just come up with an excellent plan. A way to kill two birds with one stone. If it would just work . . .

Two

Craig

I WASN'T THINKING about anything except food when I got to the pizza place that Monday night in July. I was starving. It had been a long drive from D.C. and I'd gotten a late start, thanks to my folks. Their car was out of commission, as usual—that's what they got for insisting on driving the same hunk of junk since the late seventies—and they suddenly remembered about a million errands they needed to do. As usual, they hadn't come right out and asked me to help them. But I knew if I didn't, the stuff wouldn't get done. Sometimes I'm too responsible for my own good. Conscientious Craig— that's what my parents call me. I just hoped they managed to scrape up enough responsibility between the two of them to remember to feed my dog, Mimi.

What with my flaky family and the summer traffic, it was dusk by the time I hit the Lenape

Beach town limits. And my brother, Hewitt, and his girlfriend hadn't had any food in the house when I reached the ramshackle cottage they'd rented. That was no big shock. Those two were usually too busy making out to think about much of anything else. You'd think that, having been a couple all through their first year of college, the thrill might have worn off a little. At least enough to give them time for stuff like grocery shopping.

Luckily our other housemate, Hew and Lara's friend from college, Ed, had recommended Niko's Boardwalk Pizzeria. Ed had spent the past few summers in Lenape Beach, so he knew all the best spots. At least that was what Hewitt had said on the phone a week earlier.

"It's awesome here, Craig!" Hew had exclaimed. "Great food, great beach, great parties. You'll have a blast. There are hot girls everywhere. Even *you* might be able to score!"

That was typical Hewitt and, as usual, I hadn't bothered to respond. Even though I was two years younger than Hew, I often felt like the older brother. Actually, I usually felt more like a visitor from another planet than an actual member of my own family. I was the only one of the four of us with any common sense. My brother and parents had an irritating way of taking things one day at a time, following their hearts instead of their heads, and counting on luck and good intentions. They never seemed to worry about the future or anything practical. And they needed to more than anyone—

my parents' finances were a mess, and Hew was on the verge of flunking out of college.

My parents grew up in the sixties, and I suspect they never got over it. That's no excuse, if you ask me. But Hew had even less of an excuse. I was sure he would be doing a whole lot better in school if he didn't have Lara Lips in his face twenty-four hours a day. Still, I supposed it was an improvement. In high school Hew had been a womanizer, scamming on every girl in sight without caring about any of them. At least now he was having a real, serious relationship, in his own way.

I liked pretty girls as much as the next guy, as long as they had more than looks going for them. But I didn't let them distract me from more important things, like school or work—or food, for that matter. The smell in the pizza place was making my mouth water, and I couldn't wait to get back to the cottage and relax with a few slices.

Despite all that, I noticed the blond girl immediately. I couldn't help it. The restaurant was crowded, but she stood out in a big way. She'd looked over and smiled when the guy behind the counter shouted out my order, then turned away a second later. But that second had been enough for me to see that she was incredible. In fact, I was sure she had to be the best-looking girl I'd ever seen.

I glanced at the guy sitting with her. He was a big, beefy-looking guy with a blond buzz cut. Obviously a date—maybe a boyfriend. I felt an irrational twinge of disappointment.

I shook my head, trying to shake off the feeling. Naturally the girl had caught my eye. She was amazing-looking. I would've had to be dead not to notice her. But that didn't mean anything. I wasn't looking to meet girls. That wasn't what this time at the beach was about. It was about money, plain and simple. I needed a job where I could come up with a nice chunk of cash in a short period of time.

Besides, the girl obviously wasn't my type. I'd known girls like her back in D.C., pretty, flirty girls who tossed their hair and batted their eyelashes. Most of them hadn't ever had a deeper thought than which shade of nail polish to wear to the prom. That kind of girl ended up dating Hew, not me.

But I couldn't help sneaking another glance. Something about her expression drew my eye. There was something kind and a little bit mysterious lurking behind that pretty face. Something different.

I was surprised to find her looking right back at me. She was smiling again. I smiled back tentatively.

Then, to my amazement, she leaped out of her chair and came rushing toward me. I took a step backward, wondering if she'd mistaken me for someone else. She flung her arms around me before I could say a word. Her hug almost knocked me out—she was wearing a sleeveless blouse, and her arms felt warm through my T-shirt. And her hair smelled really nice—like flowers. I couldn't think about anything else for a second. Just that smell.

The girl pulled back, keeping her hands on my arms and looking me over. She was still smiling. "Cousin Stefan!" she exclaimed loudly. "I almost didn't see you there!"

"Um, I think you've—," I began.

She didn't let me finish. She leaned forward and squeezed me tight again. That shut me up. I couldn't have spoken if my life depended on it.

"Just play along," she whispered urgently.

Now the big blond guy was coming over to join us. He gave me a suspicious look.

"Do you know this guy, Jill?" he asked.

The girl—Jill—laughed. "Of course I do," she told him. "This is my cousin Stefan. He's visiting from Europe. I'm sure I must have mentioned it, Bob."

"Well, no, you didn't," Bob said. But the suspicious look was gone. Instead, he was gazing at Jill adoringly. He had it bad for her.

I began to realize what was going on. And I didn't like it. I couldn't stand people who played manipulative little games with members of the opposite sex. And now I seemed to be some kind of pawn in whatever game this girl was playing. I opened my mouth to put an end to it. But at that moment Jill turned and gave me a wink. Just a wink, one blue-green eye dropping closed for the briefest of moments. In the depths of that eye I read humor, mischief, and something else I couldn't quite put my finger on. The wink invited me to be a part of all that, maybe to find out more. I wasn't sure why that should make me keep my mouth shut. But it did.

"I'm really sorry," Jill said. "I didn't realize Stefan would be here this early. I guess I should head home. My family will be dying to see him."

Bob looked so crestfallen that it made me cringe with pity. "Are you sure?" he asked. "I mean, maybe we could drop him off and then catch a movie—"

Jill cut him off with a firm shake of her head, her blond hair dancing in the dim light of the restaurant.

Since when did I notice things like that?

"I don't think so," Jill told Bob. "Stefan and I haven't seen each other in years. We have lots of catching up to do."

"Oh. Well, maybe we could meet up again sometime later this—"

"What was that, Stefan?" Jill said, interrupting. She looked at me expectantly.

I hadn't said a word. But it was obvious she wanted me to change the subject. "Um . . . I . . . ," I mumbled. I remembered just in time that I was supposed to be European. I tried to come up with some semblance of an accent. "I tink I am rawther tired," I blurted out, my ears turning red. I hoped Bob didn't notice. Fortunately he seemed to be completely occupied with gazing at Jill. "Uh, we can go to ze house now, pleez?"

Jill looked amused. I could guess what she was thinking: *What a dork!* "I'm really sorry," she said

16

to Bob. "I'd better go. I'll see you around, okay?"

"Okay." Bob took a step forward. He was going in for the kiss.

But Jill turned her head toward me and grabbed my arm. Before I knew it, she steered me to the end of the take-out counter, where my order was waiting. I wondered if she'd purposely avoided the kiss or if she hadn't seen it coming. I also wondered if Bob would find it strange that Stefan was picking up a pizza order so soon after his arrival.

That didn't seem to bother Jill. She smiled sweetly at the tall, swarthy man behind the counter. "Is my cousin's order ready, Niko?" she asked. "If not, step on it. We've got to bail."

The man laughed. "Anything for you, Jillie," he said. He quickly rang up the order, took my money, and slid a couple of white pizza boxes across the counter. "And for your cousin, of course," he added with a wink at me.

The guy seemed a little too amused—it made me uncomfortable. But I picked up the boxes and followed Jill toward the door anyway.

Once we were outside I stopped and faced her. "All right," I said. "Would you mind telling me what that was all about?"

She glanced back at the door. Then she took my arm and led me around the corner, away from busy Lenape Avenue, onto a quieter street lined with small, brightly painted houses. "Thanks a million for playing along," she said, giving me another wide smile.

Her smile was really something. I tried to get control of myself. I had no intention of letting my hormones take over every time a girl smiled at me. I wasn't like that back home, and I wasn't going to be like that here. Otherwise I could end up like Hewitt . . . or Jill's abandoned date.

And I still didn't know what had been going on back at the pizza place. "Who was that poor guy anyway?" I asked.

She sighed. "A blind date. My parents fixed me up with him. He's a really nice guy, but we just weren't hitting it off, and we'd been sitting there for nearly two hours already. I didn't want to hurt his feelings."

I nodded slowly. So she had been playing games, but at least she'd meant well. There were times when honesty *wasn't* the best policy. Right?

In any case, I couldn't help feeling sorry for Bob. I glanced over at Jill, trying not to let her catch me looking. She would be a dream come true for most guys, I thought as I took in her pretty face, her slim figure, her smooth skin.

But not me, I told myself firmly. Definitely not. For one thing, we'd just met, and she already had me completely bewildered. I didn't like being bewildered.

We continued to wander down the street. I had no idea where we were going; I'd lost my sense of direction. Another thing I didn't like. No question about it—this girl was *way* too distracting.

"So, should I just keep calling you Stefan?" Jill

glanced up at me. Her sea green eyes looked play-ful. "Or do you have another name?"

"Craig," I told her. "My name's Craig. Craig Miller. From Washington, D.C." I was glad I had those pizzas to carry, or else I would've had no idea what to do with my hands.

"Nice to meet you, Craig Miller," she said. "I'm Jill Gersten. From right here in Lenape Beach." She came to a stop, looking into my eyes. "I really do appreciate it. Your helping me out back there, I mean."

"No big deal." I tried not to stare as she adjusted the collar of her blouse. Tried not to wonder what she would look like in a bikini.

"No, really," she said. "I owe you one, Craig."

I could almost imagine what Hewitt would say if he were here: *Go for it, dude!* I could hear his voice in my head so clearly that I was tempted to look around for him. But I knew he was back at the cot-tage, probably sitting on the couch in the midst of his never-ending make-out marathon. Ugh. Did I really want to sit around and watch that for the rest of the summer?

I gazed back at Jill. She was distracting, all right. But perhaps a little distraction could come in handy this summer. I couldn't work all the time, could I?

I'd spent the first six weeks of vacation straining my brain with a couple of college prep courses. In six more weeks, when my senior year started back in D.C., I was going to have my hands full with school-work, college applications, and all the rest. I deserved a break. Despite those intriguing eyes, this girl wasn't anyone I could imagine ever having a serious discussion with or anything. Maybe that was better—I wouldn't have to worry about getting entangled in anything complicated. Then after the summer I could go back to D.C. with no strings attached.

"I have an idea," I said, trying to sound casual. "Why don't you pay me back by grabbing some dinner with me? Say, tomorrow night."

I was surprised by how easily the words came. Watching Hew's Mr. Smooth act all those years might have rubbed off on me. That was a scary thought.

"Sure, that would be cool," Jill replied. "But can we make it a late movie instead of dinner? I have a play rehearsal tomorrow, and I won't be finished until nine-thirty or so."

"No problem," I said. "Um, where are the movie theaters in this town?" Realizing that sounded kind of stupid, I quickly added, "I just got here today."

"Oh, really? Well, I guess I'm lucky I ran into you, then." Jill put a hand on my arm and led me toward the end of the block. I followed wordlessly. I was very aware of her skin on mine. Too aware.

Maybe this isn't such a good idea after all, I thought.

She led me around another corner and pointed to the floodlit marquee of an old-fashioned-style theater just across the street. "There," she said. "It's the only movie theater in town. One screen. If you

20

want to see anything else, you have to drive to one of the malls out on the highway."

I read the name of the movie that was playing. "I haven't seen this one yet," I said. "I'm game if you are."

She nodded and squinted at the sign over the box office. "There's a ten o'clock show," she said. "Should we meet here at a quarter of?"

It took me a while to find my way back to the rental cottage. Jill gave me such an amazing smile as we parted that I completely forgot to ask her to point me in the right direction. *Definitely* distracting. I was really starting to think I'd made a mistake.

Since when was I so impulsive? I'd never asked out a total stranger before. With all the important things I had to do, from schoolwork to part-time jobs and internships to keeping my family out of trouble, I hadn't had much time to spare on girls. But the occasional girlfriends I'd had over the years were all people I'd known for a while first—smart, sensible, accomplished girls I'd met in school or at work.

But I didn't know Jill at all.

Well, there wasn't much I could do about it now. The best thing would be not to think about it until the next night.

The cottage my brother had rented was on Sea Star Street. The neighborhood was pleasant, if not the ritziest part of town. The houses were small, and most of them hadn't been fixed up much since they'd been built, sometime in the fifties. Our place was tall and narrow, with white siding, red shutters, and a gigantic blue-flowered hydrangea bush threatening to take over the front steps. I pushed my way past the monster plant and let myself in the screen door.

"Chow's here," I called.

Footsteps came clattering down the stairs that led up to the loft bedroom. It had to be Ed. Hew and Lara were already downstairs on the couch, right where I had left them—still wrapped around each other and making out as though the world were going to end tomorrow.

I set the pizza boxes on the rickety table and gave Hewitt a kick in the shin. "Yo," I said. "Come up for air, will you? Food's here."

Lara pulled back and glanced up. "Oh, hi, Craig. Thanks for picking up the 'za." She stood and reached for the nearest box.

Hew pawed at Lara for a moment, then realized he'd lost her attention to the food. So he jumped to his feet and grabbed a slice for himself.

"Ugh," he said. "What's with the freaky toppings, dude? What are those green things?"

"Capers." I grabbed the slice out of his hand. "It's the spicy sauce special—Ed recommended it."

"That's right," Ed drawled, entering the room. "Best pizza at the beach. We ordered a plain pepperoni for you wimps."

I'd only met Ed that day, and I wasn't sure what

I thought of him. He looked like a stereotypical beach bum—tall and skinny, with a sunburned nose and wild tufts of hair that had been bleached almost white by the sun. He didn't have much to say, but he seemed to have his act together. And he was totally mellow. He had to be. He'd been living with Hewitt and Lara since the beginning of the summer, and their annoying lovey-dovey nonsense hadn't driven him crazy yet.

Hewitt flipped open the lid of the second box, and he and Lara helped themselves while I bit into the slice I'd snatched from him. It was a little cold, thanks to my long walk home, but it tasted great anyway.

"This is awesome," I mumbled around my mouthful of food.

"Told you," Ed replied lazily. He flopped onto the couch with his slice and reached for the TV remote.

I sat down in a wicker chair and leaned back with a sigh. I had to admit it felt good to be there. It had been at least half an hour since I'd thought about my parents' latest financial disaster. That had to be some kind of record. Maybe being there would help me relax. Maybe by the time I got back, the whole mess would have worked itself out. Somehow.

"Okay, who wants what?" A new voice broke into my thoughts.

I glanced up in surprise. A girl stood in the archway leading into the long, narrow kitchen at the back of the house. She held a dented metal tray loaded with beverages.

The girl was really striking. She was about five foot three, with an angular figure and sleek dark hair that came just to her chin. Her face was angular too—high cheekbones, narrow nose and chin.

Lara noticed my expression. She grinned through a mouthful of pizza and jerked her head at the other girl. "Hey, Nicole. Let me introduce you to Hewie's younger brother."

The girl gave me a quick once-over before she smiled at me. "Hi," she said, setting her tray down carefully on the wobbly table. "You must be Craig. Lara's told me all about you. I'm Nicole Baxter."

"Nicole works in my office," Lara offered, grabbing one of the glasses on the tray. Lara had landed a summer job in a local real estate business. It sounded like a really prime job—much better than the no-brain-required gigs I'd managed to find. I guessed they'd hired her because she was an accounting major.

Nicole didn't look any older than me. But I wasn't surprised that the real estate company had hired her. Her whole appearance spoke of responsibility and maturity. In contrast to the sloppy shorts and tank tops everyone else was wearing, she was dressed in a crisp button-down shirt and a khaki skirt. She looked classy. Cool. Pulled together.

I couldn't help smiling in approval as I checked her out.

"Do you want some soda?" Nicole asked.

"Thanks." I reached for the glass she offered. My fingers brushed hers as I took it.

Nicole pushed her way past the couch to the chair next to mine. She picked up a piece of pizza, then smiled at me again. Her clear brown eyes were serious and intelligent-looking. "Lara tells me you're a really good student."

"Nicole's really smart," Lara put in between chews. "And she's from D.C. too. I told her all about you. I think you two have a lot in common."

I saw Lara turn and smirk at my brother. Hewitt tossed off a casual thumbs-up, then returned to devouring his fourth slice of pizza.

I suddenly realized what was going on. This was a setup! Hew was making sure his pathetic little brother wasn't lonely at Babe Beach. Or maybe it was all Lara's idea. Either way, I didn't like it.

I felt like getting up and walking out. But Nicole seemed nice and normal, and this wasn't really her fault. It wouldn't kill me to hang out with her for a while.

". . . so I got the extra credits that way, and they let me graduate a year early." Nicole shrugged. "Georgetown, here I come."

It was half an hour later. The remains of dinner were still scattered across the table, but Nicole and I had the room to ourselves. We'd moved out of the scratchy wicker chairs onto the lumpy couch. Hew and Lara had disappeared into their bedroom off the kitchen. Ed had finished his pizza and melted away without a word.

By now I had to admit that Lara might have been on to something. I was pretty impressed by Nicole—she had goals, ambition, a real point of view about the world. And she didn't giggle and gush her way through a conversation like a lot of girls I'd known. When she had something to say she said it—plain, honest, and simple.

"So what are you doing in Lenape Beach?" I asked, swallowing back a belch. Soda always makes me burp. When we were little, Hew and I used to have competitions to see who could burp out the whole alphabet faster. Somehow I didn't think Nicole would be amused by that.

She rolled her eyes. "It wasn't my idea to come here. I actually had a shot at an internship at the Library of Congress. But my family had already decided they wanted to do the beach thing this summer. I had no choice."

I nodded. I understood all too well how parents could mess up your plans. But I didn't say so. I was afraid it would sound like whining, and Nicole didn't seem like the kind of girl who would put up with that.

Nicole changed the subject to the stock market, and that's when it hit me. Maybe this was fate kicking me in the butt. Nicole could be the girl I'd been holding out for—someone with serious plans for the future, someone as dependable and responsible and logical as I was myself. Sure, I'd been pretty attracted to Jill back at the pizza place. But I wasn't kidding myself. She came across as someone who'd be anything but dependable. I could tell myself it was the mysterious expression in her eyes that had attracted me, but that was probably just my hormones making excuses.

I glanced at Nicole out of the corner of my eye. She shifted her position on the couch and her skirt slid up to reveal a couple more inches of her legs. I gulped. She might not be quite as incredible-looking as Jill, but she wasn't bad. Not bad at all.

And looks aside, she was just what I had always told myself I wanted but never expected to find. She could be more than a girlfriend. She could be a real partner. Plus she was from D.C. and she was going to Georgetown—my first-choice college. It all made such perfect sense, fit together so logically. . . .

I decided it couldn't hurt to explore this idea further. What did I have to lose? My summer jobs promised to be the polar opposite of intellectually stimulating, and I didn't want my brain to rot. At the very least, Nicole might be someone intelligent to talk to for the next month and a half. "Hey, I haven't even been down to check out the ocean yet," I said, leaning toward her. "Do you want to go for a walk along the beach?"

She smiled. "I thought you'd never ask."

Three

Jill

AFTER LEAVING CRAIG I felt restless. Besides, I'd wanted to give Annabelle a hard time about wussing out on me. So I headed across town to the Lagoon Dinner Theater.

The layout of Lenape Beach is pretty simple. Right in the middle of town is Lenape Avenue, the main drag. It runs from the highway all the way to the boardwalk. The dozen or so blocks closest to the ocean are packed with shops and restaurants, including Niko's. The shopping district stretches out from there onto some side streets and a couple of the other avenues. Beyond that, on the north side of town, are a few big hotels and a lot of rental cottages. On the south side is the quieter residential area where my friends and I lived. It was also where a few good restaurants, a bed-and-breakfast or two, and the Lagoon Dinner Theater were located.

Annabelle's rehearsal was entertaining, as usual.

You might think it could get boring watching people rehearse the same scenes over and over again. Maybe in a typical theater it would be. But anything Mr. Dinsdale gets his hands on is far from typical. He likes to test his cast by doing strange things at rehearsals. Sometimes he has them perform their roles blindfolded. Sometimes he has them switch roles for a scene or two—he claims it helps them get a feel for the entire play and also ensures that they know all their cues. That night he made everyone act out their parts in pantomime while he read their lines aloud. That was supposed to do something for their stage presence, I think. Or maybe it was their body language. In any case, it was pretty amusing to watch.

Donna and Tim came in toward the end of the rehearsal, holding hands and looking flushed and happy. As usual, there was a split-second reality lag as my brain tried to sort out the odd sight. How long would it be before their couplehood seemed natural to me? I never had this much trouble adjusting to Annabelle's love life. She'd had several long-term relationships over the past few years, mostly with other actors from the dinner theater. But of course, none of her boyfriends had been one of our best friends. That threw everything off.

Donna and Tim grabbed a couple of seats at my table.

"Hey," I greeted them in a whisper. "How was it?"

Donna rubbed her stomach and rolled her eyes upward. "Heavenly," she whispered back, tossing her head to get her thick brown bangs out of her eyes.

Tim blinked behind his glasses and nodded. He's tall and skinny, with big brown eyes that look even bigger behind his glasses. I've known him practically since birth—our mothers are best friends. That night he was wearing a jacket and tie that I was sure he'd borrowed from his older brother. Donna looked nice too, in a pretty flowered sundress and high-heeled sandals.

"I want to hear all about it," I told them. I noticed Mr. Dinsdale shooting me an irritated look and lowered my voice still more. "Beach meeting later?"

Donna and Tim nodded. Then we all sat back to watch the rehearsal.

"Hey, Mom!" I shouted, hurrying through the back door into the kitchen. "I'm home!"

"Hi, sweetie," my mother's voice called from the living room.

My dog, Romeo, raced into the kitchen and leaped at me, panting with excitement. He's a scrappy little mixed-breed mutt I rescued from the pound when he was a puppy, and he's more devoted than any adoring boyfriend I'd ever had. Cuter too. I ruffled his fur affectionately, then reached for his leash, which was hanging near the sink.

"I'm going out!" I yelled.

At that moment my mom appeared in the

kitchen doorway, her finger marking her place in her book and her reading glasses perched precariously on the end of her nose. Her blond hair was pulled back in a loose ponytail, and little strands had escaped and floated around her face. She looked like an absentminded professor in a movie. In reality, she's the principal of the local elementary school. She split her free time pretty evenly between catching up on her reading and trying to convince my twelve-year-old brother, Jamie, to turn off his computer and get a life. She was fairly successful at the first, but the second was hopeless. Since the divorce, my family wasn't what you would call gifted in the interpersonal communication department. Mom never seemed to have any idea what to say to bring Jamie out of his silicon shell, and he never seemed interested in listening anyway. I could hear bleeping and blipping coming from the direction of his room.

"How was your date, Jillie?" my mom asked.

I snorted and bent down to hook Romeo's leash onto his collar. "Don't ask."

She laughed. "Well, you're always telling me there are plenty of other guys out there."

"And I'm right." I grinned. "Actually, I just met someone new today. We're going out tomorrow night."

"Really?" She looked surprised. "I thought you were seeing that musician tomorrow."

I liked to tell Mom about the guys I met. It was an easy way to make conversation, and it wasn't awkward, the way it would have been with some mothers. That's because my mom didn't disapprove of my wild and crazy Date-O-Rama lifestyle at all. In fact, she encouraged it. She said that if she and my father had dated around a little more before they got serious, they might have avoided the worst mistake of both their lives—namely, getting married. It always made me feel kind of weird when she said things like that, but I'd learned to stop worrying about it and just appreciate that she didn't nag me about all my dates. I hadn't even had a curfew since I'd turned sixteen the year before.

I wrapped Romeo's leash around my hand. "I am seeing Jasper tomorrow," I told her. "We're catching a movie out at the mall. But his band is playing down in Maryland at ten. He'll be long gone by the time I'm supposed to meet Craig."

Craig. I smiled as I thought about him. He was adorable. Maybe a little serious-looking—I couldn't remember if he'd actually cracked a smile the entire time we were talking—but still totally adorable. "I'll tell you all about it in the morning, okay?"

"Okay," she replied. "Tell Annabelle and Donna and Tim that I said hi."

I nodded and headed outside with Romeo bounding along in front of me. It was a little after ten o'clock, and the sky was a deep, dark, velvety blue twinkling with stars. I strolled along the quiet blocks, enjoying the breeze coming in from the ocean, letting Romeo sniff whatever he wanted along the way. My house was five blocks from the beach. I've always thought it was the perfect distance—close enough to be convenient, far enough to avoid the crowds and noise of the rentals and the boardwalk.

When I reached the cross street just before the ocean block, I turned and walked a couple of blocks south, out toward the outskirts of town. During the winter dogs are allowed on the beach, but they're banned in season. Officially, that is. Unofficially, the local cops would look the other way for a fellow townie like me if they could. But I had to be careful not to get caught by a transient who might report me. Otherwise the cops would have no choice but to fine me—and I certainly didn't need that. My part-time job didn't pay much, and Mom did all she could do to make ends meet at home. The last thing I wanted to do was ask my father for money.

So in the summer we always met on the nearly deserted stretch of beach beyond the end of the boardwalk, where the ocean dipped in toward the lake that separated Lenape Beach from the next town to the south. There were only a few big, fancy beachfront houses there, and most of them were empty most of the time.

My friends were all there when I arrived. I kicked off my shoes and let Romeo off his leash. He raced down to play in the surf.

"Howdy," Annabelle greeted me with a sheepish grin. She'd been too busy to come over and talk during the rehearsal, so we hadn't had a chance to discuss her pitiful performance at the pizza place yet.

But for some reason, being on the darkened beach in the moonlight made me feel forgiving. I dropped to the sand, which still retained a hint of heat from the sun, and stretched out on my back with my hands behind my head. "Hi," I said. I grinned to let her know that I wasn't holding a grudge. Then I turned my head toward Donna and Tim.

Tim was leaning against a dune and Donna was resting against him, her arms around his skinny chest, looking perfectly content.

"So, Jill." Donna sounded amused. "Annabelle was just starting to tell us about your big date."

I sat up. "A fat lot she knows about it," I said with a grimace. "She left me there to die of boredom. Luckily, a handsome prince came to my rescue."

"Really?" Annabelle said. "This sounds intriguing."

Tim grinned. "You're not talking about Niko, are you?"

I rolled my eyes. We all loved Niko. But he was old and fat, and not what you would call a major hunk. "Not quite," I responded. "It was a transient. He came in a few minutes after you left, Annabelle. By the way, thanks."

"Yeah, yeah." Annabelle waved her slender hands dramatically. "Enough of that. Let's hear the story."

I told them all about it, not skimping on the details. Especially the ones about how gorgeous Craig was.

There was just one detail I left out—the weird feeling I'd gotten when Craig looked at me with those deep, serious eyes of his. The feeling that he'd been seeing more of me than he should. I don't mean that in an indecent way or anything. It wasn't my body he'd been checking out—it was *me*. At least that's how it had seemed. It had felt odd, confusing, and a little scary. I wasn't sure I was ready to talk about it or even think about it. It had all probably been in my imagination anyway. My seashell-addled brain must have started spontaneously hallucinating at the thought of escaping from Babbling Bob.

When I'd finished my glowing description of Craig, Donna extricated herself from her cozy pose with Tim and sat up. "So he asked you out," she said. "And you're seeing him tomorrow night."

I nodded. "After my date with Jasper. I just hope I can make the switch from bad-girl rock-and-roll groupie to wholesome pizza gal. I'm pretty sure Craig is a brain muffin."

Donna shook her head. "I don't know how you do it," she told me. "I really don't." She snuggled back down against Tim.

"I don't either," I admitted cheerfully. "But it sure is fun."

Annabelle chuckled. "You're going to get caught one of these days, you know," she warned jokingly.

I just smiled back at her. I knew I wasn't going to get caught. And even if I did slip up someday, so what? Maybe I didn't tell my various dates about each other, but I also never pretended that any guy was my one and only either. I never let things go too far, and I never led anyone on. If I ever thought a guy was starting to get serious about me, I broke it off—fast.

"I can't believe you set up another date right after you had such a horrible time with that Bob guy." Tim looked perplexed. He was a simple soul. He never understood my dating game.

"Tim has a point," Annabelle put in. "Why didn't you just invite this Greg—"

"Craig," I corrected quickly.

Annabelle shrugged. "As if it matters," she said. "Anyway, why didn't you invite him to hang with us at the beach or something? For all you know he could be a psycho."

"Or worse yet, a seashell enthusiast," Donna teased.

"No way." I shook my head. "I got a really good feeling from this one." I paused thoughtfully. "Although it could've been gratitude for rescuing me. Who knows?"

Donna laughed. "You're too much," she said.

"Maybe," I agreed. "But if you didn't have me around, what would you guys talk about?"

"She has a point there," Annabelle said.

The subject soon changed to Donna and Tim's big dinner. As I listened I glanced out toward the ocean to check on Romeo. I picked up a handful of sand and let it run out through my fingers. In the milky dimness of the moonlight, it seemed to sparkle a little, as if there were small diamonds mixed in.

My mind was still on Craig. I knew there was definitely something different about him. Was it that serious, intense, searching look he'd given me? Or the way his muscles had tensed as I hugged him? Was it merely that divine little cleft in his chin? Or was it something much more complicated?

I shivered, even though the night was still warm. Whatever it was, I decided, I couldn't wait to find out more.

The next morning I got to work around seven. I'd been waitressing at Crabby Kate's, a casual seafood restaurant on Lenape Avenue, for a couple of years. That—plus the fact that I was a local— gave me enough seniority so that Mildred, the owner, usually let me pick my own shifts. I liked to work breakfast and lunch. Crabby Kate's was known for its killer breakfast, so the morning tips weren't bad, and it left my afternoons and evenings free. It also meant I didn't have to deal with the crowds at the twice-weekly all-you-can-eat seafood feast.

I entered through the back door and grabbed my blue crab-patterned apron off the hook. The cooks were already there, and the smell of sizzling bacon and hot coffee flavored the air.

Mildred bustled into the kitchen. Mildred's mother was the original Kate, whose husband started the restaurant back in the fifties. Now Mildred and her two sons ran the place.

"Morning, Jill," she said briskly. She yanked on the hair net that covered her gray hair. "You're late."

I yawned and glanced at my watch. I *was* late— by three and a half minutes. Mildred ran a tight ship. "Sorry," I said tiredly. "The dog ate my alarm clock."

Mildred rolled her eyes and snorted. But she smiled as she hurried off to talk to the cooks.

The restaurant was crowded that morning. I hardly had two seconds to think about my interesting evening plans. I was so busy that it took me a minute to notice Warren and Wendy Warnicki come in.

Warren and Wendy are twins, though they look nothing alike. Warren's skinny, on the short side, and has curly brown hair. Wendy's taller and bigger than her brother, and her jet-black hair is stick straight. They're both in my class at school, and I'd actually gone out with Warren a couple of times a few years earlier. I broke it off when I realized he was getting serious about me. I don't know if that's why Wendy didn't like me. But I wasn't crazy about her either. She never laughed, and the expression on her face always looked like she'd just smelled something disgusting.

I'd seen the Warnicki twins in Crabby Kate's before, so their arrival wasn't big news. What *was* major news was the guy who came in with them.

Mildred was actually the first to notice him.

"Hmmm," she said, pausing on her way out of the kitchen into the dining room. I was right behind her and I almost bumped into her well-padded behind. I caught myself just in time to avoid spilling the orange juice and coffee on my tray.

Mildred glanced back and realized she was blocking my way. She stepped aside to let me through, at the same time nodding toward the door. "You may want to check out the Viking that just walked in."

I followed her gaze and saw that Wendy and Warren were standing by the hostess station with a tall Nordic god. He was well over six feet tall and had a very muscular build. His short hair was pale blond, and even from across the room I could tell his eyes were a bright, flawless blue. "Wow," I breathed.

Mildred shot me an amused glance. "Let me take that tray," she said. "Why don't you go seat that party?"

"You're a slave driver, Mildred," I said happily, handing over my loaded tray and making tracks for the hostess station.

Wendy didn't seem very happy to see me. But Warren greeted me politely. He even introduced me to the Viking as I seated them.

"This is Olaf," he said. "Our exchange student from Norway."

I had heard the Warnickis were hosting a foreign student for the summer. But they always spent the first six weeks of the summer with relatives in

Boston, so I hadn't seen them—or Olaf—before this.

"It's nice to meet you, Olaf," I said, holding out my hand.

Olaf had already taken his seat. Now he leaped up and grasped my hand firmly. "*Ja,* is nice to meet you, Miss Jill," he responded with a heavy but adorable Scandinavian accent.

Wendy frowned and cleared her throat loudly. "Olaf doesn't speak much English," she said. "I'm sure you'll forgive him if he doesn't talk to you."

I ignored her and looked up at Olaf, who was still standing. He was also still holding on to my hand. I didn't mind. "How do you like the United States so far?" I asked, giving him my brightest smile.

He nodded a few times, looking as though he was trying to come up with the right words. "Oh, is very good," he said finally. "Very nice. This beach especially I like."

"Really?" I noticed a man at the next table waving his coffee cup at me. I decided he could wait a little longer for his free refill. "Have you seen much of the shore yet? There are lots of fun towns farther down toward Maryland."

"Murra-lind?" Olaf's forehead wrinkled and a perplexed look clouded his clear blue eyes. He had finally let go of my hand.

"Maryland," Wendy muttered. "It's a state."

"Oh, *ja,*" Olaf exclaimed. "I hear much about Murra-lind. But I not have seen it yet. Only Boston and Len-ippy Beach."

41

"Oh, but you have to see more of the area," I said smoothly. "You should take the coastal highway down to Ocean City. It's an awesome drive." I didn't know if my flirting would be able to get past the language barrier, but I figured it was worth a shot.

"Oh, yes?" Olaf paused, and once again I could almost see his mind busily translating what he wanted to say from Norwegian into English. "Then Miss Jill, might I ask you one day to show me this drive?"

I couldn't help shooting Wendy a glance. She looked more annoyed than I'd ever seen her. Warren looked a little taken aback himself.

I returned my attention to Olaf. "That sounds like fun," I told him. "I'd love to take you around."

"Olaf doesn't have a driver's license," Wendy cut in.

"That's okay," I said, smiling. "We can take my car. I'm off on Friday. Is that good for you, Olaf?"

"*Ja,*" he replied. "Friday for me is very good."

"Great. I'll pick you up at noon. We can grab some lunch on the way." Wendy was still glowering. I decided to make my escape before she exploded. "Well, you've got your menus," I told them. "The specials are on the board over the register. I'll send someone over to take your order."

I raced back into the kitchen, eager to share my triumph with Mildred. Was I good, or what?

Four

Craig

I STARTED THE first of my two part-time jobs on Tuesday morning. I was still kind of bummed about not finding anything full-time. The jobs I'd managed to land weren't exactly going to knock anybody's socks off on my college applications. But I'd been lucky to get anything at all so late in the summer. And at least the pay was decent—that was my main concern at this point. All the brilliant college applications in the world weren't going to help much if I didn't have the cash to pay for tuition when the bursar's bills started coming.

The second job was at a candy store. But the first job was at one of those weird little places that seem to exist only at the beach or other types of tourist traps—one of those stores where people get dressed up as cowboys or pirates or whatever and then have their picture taken with one of those cameras that make everything look grainy and old-fashioned.

Business was slow at first, so I had plenty of time to think about the two girls I'd met the previous day.

Nicole and I had spent a lot of time walking along the beach the night before, talking about our schoolwork and our goals for the future. She really had it together—she'd already decided what she wanted to do with her life and how to go about it, right down to which law school she wanted to attend after she graduated from Georgetown. It was really impressive. Next to her, I almost felt like a slacker.

Eventually I had walked her back to the house her family was renting. She'd stopped me as we reached the front steps.

"I like you, Craig," she said, putting a hand on my arm. "I had my doubts when Lara wanted me to come meet you. But I'm glad I did."

"Same here," I told her. And I meant it too—Nicole wasn't like any girl I'd ever met. But I wasn't sure what to say next. Now that we weren't talking about safe subjects such as school and money and jobs, my mind was suddenly drawing a blank. "Um, maybe we can get together again soon."

"I'd like that," she said. "Have you heard about this Full Moon Fever thing next week?" I shook my head, and she explained. "It's some kind of after-dark beach party that's held each month during the full moon. I missed the last one, but I heard it's fun. It's next Monday night. Would you like to go?"

"Sure," I said, relieved that she had taken the lead. "That sounds cool."

"Great." She seemed to expect me to do or say something after that. I did the only thing I could think of: I leaned over and kissed her good-night. She kissed me back for a few seconds before pulling away. Then she said good-bye and headed inside.

I had watched the front door close behind her, feeling an odd twinge of disappointment. It had been a while since I'd kissed a girl, but somehow I'd remembered it being a little more exciting.

Now, lost in thought at my new job, I shook my head, feeling annoyed with myself. Why did I always have to be so critical? The kiss had been fine. I shouldn't have expected major passion and fireworks—after all, Nicole and I had just met.

But a stray thought flitted through my brain. *I'll bet Jill doesn't kiss like that.*

Jill. I shook my head. Now that I'd met Nicole, I'd be better off forgetting all about Jill. What had attracted me to her anyway? A mysterious expression in her pretty eyes, a warm, fuzzy feeling I'd gotten from her smile? That inane stuff couldn't compare to the respect and admiration I already felt for Nicole. I'd known from the beginning that Jill wasn't my type. She was carefree and flirtatious and probably completely shallow and frivolous. The ridiculous scene in the pizza place had pretty much shown that she was into playing games. Yes, I was fairly certain that my first date with Jill would also be our last.

The little bell over the door rang, startling me out of my thoughts. My boss, an older man with white hair and a weather-beaten face, stood up quickly as a whole group of girls poured into the shop. They looked about twelve and they all were giggling.

I tried to help as my boss talked them into getting a photo taken and herded them toward the costume rack.

"He's cute," I heard one of the girls whisper loudly to her friend. They all turned to stare at me and started giggling louder than ever.

I felt my cheeks burn with embarrassment.

"This way, girls!" My boss did his best to be heard over the laughter. "The costume racks are back there."

After a fifteen-minute discussion of who would look best in what, the girls selected their costumes and swept back toward the dressing rooms en masse. My boss collapsed in his chair again and mopped his brow.

"Women," he muttered. "They're nothing but trouble. Even at that age."

I nodded in agreement. I knew exactly what he meant.

I arrived at the movie theater a few minutes early that night. Not because I was eager to see Jill—by now I had convinced myself that this date was just a chore I had to get out of the way. No, it was because I had to get out of the cottage before the crazy kissers drove me wacko.

The sun had set some time ago, but the streets of downtown Lenape Beach were still bustling. People went in and out of restaurants, bought tickets at the theater, strolled along the sidewalk, or just hung out in the warm, breezy summer night. I purchased a pair of tickets, then leaned against the brick wall of the theater to wait.

And wait. Our meeting time came and went. Jill didn't show.

I waited some more. As the hands on my watch crept forward slowly, I felt more and more irritated. I should have known Jill was the type of girl who would be late. The type who wouldn't take anything seriously or care that other people might have important things to do or schedules to keep. Talk about irresponsible.

Soon there were less than five minutes until the movie started. I glanced at my watch again and decided that if she wasn't there by show time, I was going to bail.

"Craig!" a breathless voice called.

I looked up—Jill was hurrying across the street toward me. Instantaneously my aggravation faded away to nothing. I'd almost forgotten how beautiful Jill was.

She paused to let a pickup full of college kids roar past, then jogged the rest of the way to me. Her face was flushed pink and her long blond hair was windblown and disheveled. I liked her hair that way.

"Sorry I'm late," she said, gasping for breath.

"My rehearsal ran later than I thought. And I couldn't sneak out—um, I'm the lead." She hesitated a little before she said that, as if she were too shy to admit it.

"Really?" I asked. Even though she'd mentioned the play the night before, it hadn't really sunk in. I hadn't pegged her as the actress type. "That's great. What play are you doing?"

"*My Fair Lady,*" she replied. "It's just a local dinner theater, but we have fun. Anyway, I really am sorry I kept you waiting."

"It's okay." I surprised myself at how easily I forgave her, considering how annoyed I'd been mere seconds earlier. But somehow just seeing her standing in front of me was apology enough.

It was more than enough. I couldn't take my eyes off her. I devoured the sight of her, taking in the hint of tanned skin visible beneath her cropped top and the way her faded blue jeans hugged every curve. But my gaze soon returned to her eyes. I hadn't been imagining things the night before. Her eyes were incredible.

I did my best to drag myself back to sanity. I couldn't stand there gaping at her all night. She'd be sure to notice. I forced myself to speak. "I have our tickets," I said, amazed that my voice came out sounding normal. "We still have time to catch the previews."

We went inside and found seats just before the lights dimmed. I was glad the movie was about to start. It meant we wouldn't have to try to make conversation, and I wasn't sure I'd be able to speak coherently quite yet.

Something very strange was going on here, and it scared me a little. Okay, a *lot*. I'd never had this kind of immediate chemical reaction to anyone before. It just didn't make sense. There was no logical reason that merely being in this girl's presence should turn my mind into mush. I didn't even know her.

But as we sat there in the darkened theater I couldn't stop thinking about how close Jill was to me. I could hear every rustle her clothing made as she moved. And that incredible scent I'd noticed the night before was drifting over toward me. Was it her shampoo? Her perfume? Whatever it was, it made me want to move closer. I was itching to put my arm around her.

I held myself back. Maybe I couldn't control what I was feeling, but I could certainly remain in control of my actions. I'd keep myself from acting without thinking, doing something stupid that I would end up regretting. I couldn't just turn into Hewitt—or my parents—and let my emotions rule over my common sense. I'd seen where that could lead.

I forced myself to look at the whole situation rationally, to think about Nicole. I'd already decided she was the one I was serious about. She was all pluses, no minuses—well, except for that less-than-awesome kiss. That was probably all in my head anyway.

Then there was this virtual stranger sitting

beside me. Sure, she was gorgeous. And she seemed nice. But just look at what she was doing to me. Her very presence turned me into a blithering idiot.

I was so confused, I felt as though my head were about to explode. I tried to forget about Jill and Nicole and just concentrate on the movie, but that was impossible. Besides, by this point I couldn't even follow the movie—I had no idea what it was about.

Finally I got tired of fighting it out in my mind. I felt slightly ridiculous for admitting it, even to myself, but whatever weird magnetic connection— real or imagined—was pulling me toward the girl in the next seat, it was just too strong. I had to at least give her a chance. I was sure my rational self would win out and I'd end up with Nicole. But I needed to be sure I was making the right choice.

Reaching a decision, if you could call it that, made me feel a little calmer. By the time the movie ended, I was breathing almost normally again. Jill and I stood and made our way to the exits with the rest of the audience. We stepped outside, the air feeling hot and muggy after the air-conditioned theater.

"What did you think of the movie?" she asked, tipping her head back to look at me. The moon-light caught her eyes, making them look more blue than green.

"Uh . . ." *Movie? What movie?* "It was okay, I

guess. Hey, are you hungry? Maybe we could grab a bite somewhere."

She smiled. "Sure. But I can't stay out too late. I have to be at work early tomorrow."

I glanced at my watch. It was almost midnight, and I had to be at the photo place first thing in the morning as well. "A quick bite, then," I agreed.

A few minutes later we were seated at an out-door table at a place on the boardwalk called the Sea Shanty. Music was playing inside the open-air building, which was little more than a glorified lean-to. Where we were sitting, the sound of the surf drowned out the music.

A waitress came over and we ordered sodas and fries. When the waitress left to get our food, it was suddenly as if my brain had dried up and blown away, or as if I had changed into someone who had been raised by wolves and never learned to speak. I couldn't think of a single thing to say.

I stared at Jill across the table. The ocean breeze lifted individual strands of her hair and the light out there was just bright enough to illuminate the greenish blue depths of her eyes. A new feeling came over me. It was almost a depression—it suddenly seemed that there wasn't nearly enough time in the world to say everything I needed to say to her or hear everything I wanted her to tell me. It was also a feeling of frustration, since seconds were ticking by and I seemed physically incapable of saying a single word.

Jill shifted in her seat and glanced at me uncertainly. She seemed to be waiting for me to take the lead. I wanted to make her feel comfortable, to convince her that I was worth knowing. That I was witty. Fun. Interesting.

"Uh . . . so what time do you have to be at work?" I blurted out lamely.

She looked a little surprised. I felt like pounding my head on the table. What kind of idiotic question was that? So much for impressing her.

"I'm supposed to be there by seven," she replied. "It's pretty harsh. But at least I'm done early." She hesitated, then smiled. "Um, still, I can't wait for Friday—my day off."

"Cool," I said. I wasn't exactly sure what was cool about it. But I had to say something. I tried to think of a more interesting topic. "So tell me about that play you're in. You must be a good actress if you got the lead."

Her eyes darkened. "I guess," she said shortly. "Like I said, it's just a local production. No big deal."

An awkward silence fell over us. I couldn't understand what was happening. Back there in the movie theater, I'd almost convinced myself that this girl and I had some kind of special connection. Now we couldn't even manage to carry on a conversation for more than two sentences. That's what I got for making decisions based on vague feelings and weird sensations instead of common sense and logic.

Finally the waitress returned. "Here you go." She distributed our sodas and plunked the fries down in the middle of the table. "Can I get you anything else?"

"No, thanks, Mimi," Jill said, pulling her soda toward her.

The waitress nodded and hurried off. I couldn't help grinning despite the awkwardness. "Her name's Mimi?"

Jill nodded. "She goes to my school," she said. "Why?"

"Oh, nothing." I already regretted saying anything. Now she was going to think I was weird on top of everything else. "It's just that my dog's name is Mimi."

Jill's face lit up. It was amazing. Just a moment before, she'd been staring at her soda as though she were trying to melt the ice with her eyes. Now she was smiling and begging me to tell her all about Mimi.

And just like that, the awkwardness was gone. We chatted about Mimi for a while, then Jill told me about her dog, Romeo. She had all kinds of funny stories about him. Her eyes sparkled when she talked about him, and her expression was completely guileless, full of a really pure kind of happiness that I'd rarely seen before in anyone over the age of four.

Before I knew it, I was reaching for the last fry in the basket. I had no idea how much time had passed. "Dogs are the best, aren't they?" I said, licking some salt off my fingers. I hadn't felt this relaxed and happy in ages.

Jill nodded and sipped her soda. "They're incredible." She looked at me shyly. "I think one reason humans love them so much is because we're jealous of them. Dogs are so simple and genuine. You never have to wonder where you stand with a dog—they don't have a deceptive or secretive bone in their bodies."

I'd never thought about it that way. I was impressed—Jill definitely wasn't as shallow and silly as I'd first thought. But I wasn't sure how to express that to her without sounding like a dork. "Romeo sounds pretty cool," I told her instead.

"Oh, he is," she assured me. "You've got to meet him sometime. Maybe we could get together again later this week and I could bring him along."

It took me a second to realize that she had just asked me out. But I didn't have to think too hard for an answer—I *had* to see her again. This was a new and different kind of feeling for me, the king of self-control.

I couldn't help but go with it. "Sure," I agreed. "That would be great. Maybe we could hang out on Friday. I don't have to work. You said that's your day off too, right?"

She didn't say anything for a second. "Um, I can't do it then," she said at last. "I mean, it is my day off. But I already have plans."

"Oh." I was surprised at how disappointed I felt. I had already started imagining it—spending the whole day hanging out at the beach with Jill.

"It's just a family thing," she added quickly.

"Actually, um, it's my parents' twenty-fifth-anniversary party. I wish I could get out of it, but there's no way. My relatives are coming in from all over the country, and we hired a band and a caterer and everything. It will probably last all day." She laughed weakly. "Believe me, I'd much rather hang out with you. Who wants to spend a gorgeous summer day strapped into a puffy dress drinking tea with my fat old aunts?"

"It's okay," I said. "I understand. How about Saturday?" I suggested. "We could have dinner."

"Saturday's good," she said. "But I can't do dinner—play rehearsal. How about lunch instead?"

"All right." I would have to juggle my work schedule a bit. But that wouldn't be a big deal. "Saturday lunch is cool."

A little later I walked Jill home through the darkened streets. She lived across town from where I was staying. It was well after midnight and her neighborhood was quiet. It was quite a change from Sea Star Street, where the partying seemed to go on all night. I guessed it was more of a year-round family neighborhood. Jill and I walked slowly, talking in low voices. She pointed out a few town landmarks as we walked.

I tried to concentrate on what Jill was saying. But I kept getting distracted by my own thoughts— about her.

Jill was everything I *wasn't* looking for. Lighthearted. Playful. Carefree. I seriously doubted she had a five-year plan like Nicole's. Or that she would understand the things I worried about late at night as I tried to fall asleep.

Did that matter? *Of course it does,* I told myself. But I wasn't completely convinced.

Jill stopped in front of a yellow house in the middle of one of the sleepy blocks. "Well, here I am," she said. "Home sweet home. Thanks for walking me back."

"You're welcome," I said, looking up at her house. It was two stories high, with a tiny but colorful front yard full of flowers. I wondered which room was Jill's, and what it looked like inside.

"Okay," she said. "Um, well, I had fun tonight." She was standing a couple of feet in front of me, her back to the small front walk leading to her porch.

"Me too." Suddenly the awkwardness that I had felt earlier that night returned. I cleared my throat nervously, trying to think of something witty to say. "Um . . ." I glanced down for a second as I wiped my clammy hands on my shorts. I caught a glimpse of Jill's blond head moving closer to me. But by the time I looked up, she'd taken a few steps back.

"Okay," she said again. "Well, I guess I'll see you Saturday."

"Um, okay," was all I could manage to say in response. I suddenly realized that Jill had been waiting for me to kiss her good-night. *I'm such an idiot!* I thought miserably.

Now it was too late—Jill had turned and hurried into the house.

I was mentally kicking myself as I headed back toward the boardwalk. All of a sudden a long, brisk walk along the beach seemed like a good idea. There was no way I would have been able to fall asleep right then. I was too busy imagining what that kiss would have been like.

Five

Jill

I KNEW I'D almost blown it with Craig.

Normally that wouldn't be a big deal. I'd had off nights before. Nights when I hadn't felt like being my usual engaging and charming self. But this was different. Craig had thrown me for a loop. I hadn't been able to flirt with him in my usual effortless way, or even to make basic small talk. It was as if I couldn't quite figure out which of my roles to play with him. But why?

Craig was different. That was the easy answer. But what exactly was it about him? Was it the way he'd listened so intently to everything I said? The way he'd looked at me with those serious green eyes of his? Or was it the way I'd felt when we finally connected, when we really began to talk to each other? For a few minutes there it hadn't seemed as if I was on a date at all. It was more like being with my best friends, just talking comfortably and being myself.

That was definitely a scary thought. Craig was a transient, a stranger. Was I letting his handsome face go to my head? I tried to shrug it off as I climbed into bed that night, telling myself I was silly to make such a big deal out of the situation.

But it was still bugging me the next afternoon when I left work and headed for the Lagoon Dinner Theater. Opening night of *My Fair Lady* was only a week and a half away, and Mr. Dinsdale had called for a few extra rehearsals. I was supposed to meet Donna and Tim at the theater to cheer Annabelle on.

Donna and Tim were waiting for me at our usual table. Annabelle was there as well. "Hey, what's going on?" I asked her. "Didn't the rehearsal start yet?"

Annabelle rolled her eyes. "Don't ask. Mr. Dinsdale had one of his creative brainstorms. He's making each cast member act out their part all alone."

I looked up at the stage. Roger, the good-looking college student from California who was playing Freddy, walked onto the stage. He noticed us watching him and gave us a grin and a wink. Then he started acting out his part as Mr. Dinsdale observed from the wings.

Donna shook her head, smiling, as Roger carried on a conversation with the thin air. "Sometimes I think these rehearsals are better than the play itself," she remarked.

"I *always* think that," Tim put in. "It's like experimental theater or something."

Mr. Dinsdale turned around and shot us a dirty

look. He was too far away to have heard what Tim had said. He just wanted us to shut up.

"Well, since you're obviously not going to be needed for a while," I whispered to Annabelle, "why don't we all go someplace where we can talk?"

Annabelle nodded and led the way. Soon we were hanging out in the lobby and I was telling the others about my dates.

". . . so Jasper spent at least twenty minutes trying to get me to come down and see his band after the movie," I complained. "By the time I convinced him to drop me off at home, he was late for his gig and I had to run all the way downtown to meet Craig."

"Ah, yes," Donna remarked. "Craig, the mystery pizza man. How was that?"

I sighed. "Well, good and bad."

"Give us the good parts first," Tim suggested.

"No!" Annabelle protested. "I might have to go back in any minute. And I want to hear the juicy stuff."

I frowned at her. But I did what she wanted anyway, trying to put into words everything I'd been thinking since Craig and I had parted ways.

"Interesting," Annabelle said thoughtfully when I'd finally wound down. "So what does this mean? Are you seeing him again or not?"

I nodded. "I was afraid he'd say no because I was acting like such a dork there for a while. But—"

"Wait a minute," Donna interrupted. "*You* were afraid *he* would say no? Does that mean you asked him out?"

"Whoa," Annabelle said quickly. "Good catch, Donna."

I hadn't really thought about that before.

Annabelle and Donna grinned, but Tim looked puzzled. "So she asked him out. What's the big deal?" he asked.

Donna whacked him on the shoulder. "Get real! How long have you known Jill? Don't you know that the *guy* always asks *her* out? It never happens the other way around. It's like a law of nature or something."

Annabelle crossed her arms over her chest and smirked. "Well, well," she said. "After all this time. You finally met your match."

"Oh, come on," I protested. "It's not like that. I think I was just tired. You know, from all that running. And my date with Jasper."

But I didn't sound convincing even to myself. What was happening to me? I never asked guys out. I never had to. The ones I wanted always ended up asking me.

"What is it about this guy anyway?" I muttered in frustration.

I guess I muttered it a little too loudly, because Annabelle raised one of her perfectly shaped auburn eyebrows and Donna's face broke into a smile.

"She's actually falling for someone," Donna said, sounding like a proud mother sending her child off to kindergarten.

Annabelle nodded and rolled her eyes theatrically. "It's about time!"

"Oh!" Tim said, looking delighted. "I get it. She really likes this one. That's great!"

"Hel-*lo!*" I exclaimed. "Quit talking about me in the third person, okay? And for your information, I hardly even know this guy yet. All that stuff I just told you was probably all in my head."

"You don't have to explain yourself to us," Donna said dramatically. "We've all been in love. We're just happy to think that it might finally be happening for you. But don't let us rush things. You're the only one who can decide if this guy's the one."

I looked at her and frowned. Just because she and Tim were suddenly all cuddly and snuggly exclusively with each other, that didn't mean I wanted to be the same way, with Craig or any other guy. What made her think I was even interested in finding "the one," if such a creature existed?

I glanced at Annabelle. She wasn't much better. She liked to play it cool. But beneath it all, I knew she totally bought into all the happily-ever-after endings of those plays she acted in. That was why she'd accepted Donna and Tim's relationship more easily than I had. And why she jumped into a new long-term romance every chance she got.

Donna didn't notice my disgruntled expression. "So, Jill," she said. "When are you going to see him again?"

"Saturday afternoon," I said, trying to sound nonchalant. "After I go out with Olaf on Friday afternoon. And just before I go see Jasper's band play on Saturday night."

Annabelle let out a sigh and went to peek inside to see if Mr. Dinsdale was ready for her. Donna and Tim looked frustrated.

"But Jill," Tim protested, "it sounds as though you really like Craig. Shouldn't you cool it a little with all those other guys?"

I shrugged. "Why should I? It's not like he's going to know about them or anything."

"Come on, Jill," Donna said, sounding more like a parent than ever. Or a psychologist, for that matter. "You'll have to stop playing games if you want him to take you seriously. In a real relationship, honesty is the best policy."

Tim smiled and gave her shoulders a squeeze. She turned to kiss him on the tip of his nose.

I snorted, annoyed with them. Where did the likes of Donna and Tim get off giving me dating advice? They'd never even dated anyone except each other. I knew what I was doing. I was the master of this game.

"I'd better get back in there," Annabelle said. "It's almost my turn."

"I'll come with you," I told her. "I'm tired of talking."

Donna and Tim followed us back inside, their arms entwined around each other. I did my best to ignore them. Part of me felt stupid for getting so worked up. They meant well. And this thing with Craig was no big deal. Just business as usual.

Roger was finishing his one-man rendition of *My Fair Lady* as we walked in. The rest of the cast, scattered among the tables in the audience, applauded lazily as he took a bow.

"Thank you, thank you!" he exclaimed, jogging over to the edge of the stage and dropping gracefully into the orchestra pit.

I watched him walk up the aisle toward us. He was slender and tall, though not quite as tall as Craig. His shoulders weren't quite as broad as Craig's either. . . .

I caught myself and frowned. What was I doing? Had Craig taken over my mind completely? Or was my friends' brainwashing taking hold? Either way, I didn't like it.

I concentrated on just how hot Roger was. Actually, I'd noticed him before. I'd just been too busy lately to act on it. But now I was in the mood for a little acting. I wanted to prove to my friends that I wasn't losing my touch. And I had to put a stop to this obsession I was developing with Craig.

"What did you think, guys?" Roger asked as he reached us.

"Bravo," Annabelle drawled. "A spellbinding performance."

Roger laughed. "Nice try. I saw the four of you heading for the hills as soon as I came onstage. If I didn't have such a healthy ego, I might feel bad about that."

"Don't," I told him in my best flirting voice. I leaned forward, pretending I was about to reveal a deep, dark secret. Roger was an actor; I figured he'd probably like a little drama. "We just had to step outside and regain our composure so we wouldn't be overwhelmed by your incredible talent."

Roger laughed and stood close to me as Annabelle headed for the stage and Donna and Tim wandered away toward the nearest table. We were near the back of the room, so Roger and I continued to talk in low tones as Annabelle began her first scene.

And Annabelle was only halfway through scene two when Roger gave me a rakish grin and said, "So, are you busy Friday night?"

I smiled at him. Roger was suave and witty and talented. Why hadn't I gotten to know him before this? And why had I let myself think—even just for a moment—that Craig was somehow different from all the other guys I'd liked over the years? The very idea went against everything I stood for.

"I am now," I told Roger. "What do you want to do?" I shot Donna a triumphant look. I hoped she had overheard.

I still had it!

Six

Craig

"COME ON, LITTLE brother," Hewitt crowed, tipping back his chair. "When are you going to tell us about your hot night with girl number two? Don't leave us in suspense."

It was around noon, two days after my date with Jill. I'd just come home from my morning shift at my second job at the boardwalk candy shop and found Hewitt and Lara eating a late breakfast. They'd both called in sick and slept late. Typical.

Lara was leaning against the counter eating a bagel. "Yeah, let's hear it, Don Juan," she said dryly. She didn't approve of my latest date. She wanted me to hook up with Nicole and keep her and Hewitt company on the couch for the rest of the summer.

Ed was in the kitchen too, peering into the refrigerator as if it contained the meaning of life. It didn't, of course. It didn't even contain much in the way of food. But Ed managed to dig up a beer. He popped the top and sat down at the table without a word.

The phone rang. Hewitt grabbed it, then handed it to me. "It's for you," he said, waggling his eyebrows at me and smirking. "It's a gi-i-i-i-irl!"

I took the phone, suddenly feeling very nervous. *Which girl?* "Hello?"

"Hi, Craig, it's Nicole."

"Oh, hi, Nicole," I said, feeling slightly let down.

Lara sat up straight and stared at me, smiling encouragingly. Hewitt started making kissing noises. Ed just drank his beer and kept quiet.

I tried to stretch the phone cord around the corner into the living room for privacy. But in a house that size, there was only so far you could go.

"I've been thinking about you," Nicole said.

"Really?" I said. "Um, I mean, me too. I've been thinking about you."

That was the truth. Both of my mindless jobs gave me a lot of time to think. And at the moment I had only two major things on my mind. The first, of course, was the mess back home. But I didn't want to think about that too much. So I spent most of the day thinking about the second thing—my love life. I was deeply bummed out about not making a move on Jill. I couldn't seem to get it out of my mind.

I was still surprised that I'd ended up having such a good time with Jill. She wasn't my type. I could see that clearly. But she made me feel good. And then there were those eyes, of course.

Was that anything to base a relationship on, though? Whenever I'd imagined a special woman in my future, she had been a lot more like Nicole than like Jill. Nicole was smart. Interesting. Accomplished. I could picture myself with her so easily—she would fit into my life without upsetting any of my plans or goals. And I liked her.

That reminded me—Nicole was still talking on the other end of the line. I had to snap out of it. She was suggesting that we get together the next day.

"Tomorrow night?" I repeated. An image of Jill flashed in front of me and I hesitated. But my logical mind was telling me not to do anything stupid, such as write off a great girl like Nicole because of some weird, jumbled feelings. "Okay," I told her. "Tomorrow's good."

Seven

Jill

"**Y**EEE-*HA!*" OLAF RAISED his arms above his head and let the wind run through his fingers. He turned to me and grinned. "How was, Jill? Am I sound like real American now?"

I smiled back. "You bet," I assured him. "They won't recognize you back in Norway."

We were cruising down the coastal highway in my sporty little red convertible. The car had been a guilt gift from my father on my sixteenth birthday. I got a lot of great guilt gifts from him since the divorce. Buying stuff was a lot easier for him than dealing with me on any kind of meaningful level.

Olaf and I were on our way back to Lenape Beach. We'd driven down to Ocean City, Maryland, and hung out on the boardwalk there. Olaf had been incredibly sweet all day. He kept trying to win me prizes at the sideshow games. A teddy bear, a felt cowboy hat, and a giant stuffed carrot were in the backseat right now. The carrot was a little chewed—Romeo had mistaken it for a doggy toy.

It should have been the perfect day of fun in the sun. But all sorts of weird feelings kept getting in the way, keeping me from enjoying myself. I felt restless and impatient all afternoon, though I did my best to hide it from Olaf. Suddenly my little role-playing dating games felt shallow and pointless. I remembered my conversation with Craig and wondered what it would be like to be that open and natural with all of my dates.

By the time we headed for home I was getting fed up with my own stupid musings. It was probably just the language barrier that was making this outing more difficult than usual. Why would I want all my dates to be the same? The way I did it was much more interesting. I could have silly, giddy, completely lighthearted fun with Olaf, playing games and teaching him new English words. And I could act the part of a sophisticated grown-up that evening, meeting Roger for dinner at a quiet little restaurant. Then there was Jasper, the gorgeous, brooding musician. I could go watch his band play and throw myself into that whole hip, crazy scene. I could be whoever I wanted to be, get to know all sorts of different worlds. That was what I liked about dating.

I sighed and pushed my sunglasses a little farther up on my nose, trying to ignore my swirling thoughts as we neared the Lenape town limits.

"These glasses, they are very attractive on your

face," Olaf said in his accented English.

I smiled and kept my eyes on the road. "Thanks, Olaf."

I turned down the Warnickis' street. Wendy had been very adamant about demanding Olaf's return before six o'clock, so I didn't even have to make an excuse to get away in time for my date with Roger. In fact, after Olaf had kissed me sweetly and gone inside, I found myself with time on my hands.

And that was the last thing I needed. If I didn't find a way to distract myself from my own thoughts, I would go crazy.

I quickly touched up my lip gloss, which had been smudged by Olaf's kiss. It had been a nice enough kiss, nothing special. I wondered what it would be like to kiss Craig. I still could hardly believe he hadn't made a move the other night. For a second I wished I had canceled my date with Olaf that day. If I had, Craig and I could have spent the entire day at the beach together. Maybe then I would have been able to figure out why he kept popping into my mind every other second.

I turned the key and my car roared to life. The weather was so nice that I couldn't resist the urge to cruise around town for a few minutes. "What do you say, Romeo?" I pulled away from the curb. "Feel like riding around a little more?"

Romeo looked at me and gave one short bark before returning his attention to the world moving by outside the car.

"I'll take that as a yes," I said as I shifted into third.

I headed for Lenape Avenue and joined the steady line of traffic crawling down one side of the loop toward the turnaround just above the boardwalk. It was a beautiful, sunny day, and tons of people were out wandering along the avenue, shopping or eating or just enjoying the scene.

I was almost to the intersection at Myrtle Street when the light turned red. The Jeep ahead of me floored it and shot through, but I let my car glide to a stop. I was in no hurry. I watched as people poured off the sidewalks on both sides and hurried across the street. As usual, I idly checked the crowd for any cute guys.

It didn't take me long to spot one. I froze in shock. It was Craig!

Maybe it was simply because I hadn't expected to see him just then. But the sight of him, the fact of his presence, filled my entire field of vision, until the throngs of people around him faded away to nothing.

Part of me was thrilled to see him. But a more practical part was horrified. I was supposed to be somewhere else at that moment; I was sure I had come up with some sort of story when I'd made my excuses. What was it? "Uh-oh, Romeo," I whispered. "Major crisis moment."

I was tempted to duck down behind the steering wheel. But it was too late. He'd already spotted me.

He looked surprised for a second. His face had been closed-looking and serious when he started across the street. But now his expression lightened, and his lips twitched into a smile as he headed toward me. The sudden change made my heart flutter in a very strange and disturbing way.

I prayed for the light to change quickly. But I knew it wasn't going to happen. That intersection was famous for endless reds.

"Hi, Jill," Craig said when he reached my car. He leaned over the passenger-side door of the convertible to pat my dog, who went crazy at the attention, as usual. "This must be the world-famous Romeo."

I smiled weakly. "The one and only."

Craig scratched Romeo behind the ears and smiled at me. "I thought you had that anniversary thing today."

The anniversary party! That was it. What had made me come up with such a stupid story?

Craig was looking me over, confused. I realized that in my cutoff jean shorts and bikini top, I didn't look like a girl who'd been spending the day at her parents' anniversary party.

I blurted out the first thing that came into my head. "Um, I do," I said. "I mean, I'm supposed to be there right now. The party is going great—everyone's there, and Mom and Dad are dancing up a storm and having the time of their lives. I just had to slip out and take Romeo to the vet."

I realized that didn't really explain the outfit. But just as I had hoped, the story distracted Craig immediately.

"The vet?" Concern filled his green eyes. "What's

wrong with the little guy? Nothing serious, I hope."

He looked so sweet and sensitive and genuinely worried that I started to feel guilty. "No, no," I said quickly. "Um, he was stung by a jellyfish. On his paw. But he's going to be fine. He feels better already, see?" I added that last part because Romeo was looking decidedly healthy as he jumped up and down on the seat, panting happily at Craig.

I decided it was time to change the subject, pronto, before Craig pressed for details.

"You're looking awfully snazzy," I said lightly. It was true. Craig was wearing neatly pressed khakis and a polo shirt. The outfit looked great on him. "Where are you off to this evening?"

Eight

Craig

FOR A MOMENT I had no idea what to say. I was still reeling from running into Jill. My initial surprise at seeing her had quickly changed into delight. But now, as I realized the stickiness of the situation, I was feeling less delighted by the second. Even though I still wasn't sure exactly what my feelings for Jill meant, the last thing I wanted to admit to her was that I was seeing another girl. I wondered if I should pretend to have a coughing fit or something. I could try to delay long enough for the light to change. Then she would have to drive off, and I could continue on to Nicole's place.

Was this really me standing here in this awkward situation? Me—the guy who never had time for one girl, let alone two? The guy who cared more about his chemistry grade than his chemistry with the ladies? I really needed to sit down and think this one out before I started to morph into Hew or something.

But first I had to answer her question—the light didn't seem to be in any hurry to change. What was it again? Oh, right. The outfit. How was I going to explain that?

"Um, I'm on my way to dinner," I said. "With—with my boss." The lie slipped out before I could stop it. I immediately felt horrible. But what else could I have said? *The truth is, Jill, I had a fantastic time with you the other night, but now I'm on my way to pick up a girl who's much more appropriate for me in every way.* Yeah, right.

"Really?" Jill said. "Where do you work?"

"The candy store on the boardwalk."

Jill smiled. "You mean the Sugar Shop?" she asked. "Then you must work for Mrs. Mackin. She lives down the street from me." Her smile faded slightly and her smooth forehead creased into a puzzled expression. "Did you say you're having dinner with her?"

I nodded, feeling like the world's biggest idiot. No wonder I was always spouting off about being honest. It was because I couldn't lie my way out of a paper bag. "Um, yeah," I said. "That's right." I also felt like the world's biggest rat. Jill was still giving me that gorgeous smile of hers. The kind of smile a scum like me definitely didn't deserve.

Fortunately the light finally turned green. Jill glanced up, then yanked Romeo back into the car. The dog had decided he liked me and was trying to clamber out onto my shoulder. "I'd better go," Jill said apologetically. "I'll see you tomorrow, right? I'll call you at the Sugar Shop to fix a time."

"Great." I waved for a moment as she drove off. Then I smacked myself in the forehead. I was such a jerk!

I was still stewing about it as I turned onto Nicole's block. What was I going to do? I couldn't go on like this. It wasn't fair to the two girls. And it was giving me an ulcer.

Once again I weighed the options, making one last attempt to be rational and objective about it. There was Nicole. She was smart and savvy and she knew what she wanted. She was just what I would have come up with if I'd been a modern-day Dr. Frankenstein, inventing the perfect girl for myself.

Then there was Jill. She was completely inappropriate. Geographically undesirable. Totally confusing. But that didn't change the way I felt about her. I thought about her all the time. I wanted to know everything about her. The memory of her smile or her frown or the way she pushed her hair back made my heart flip over.

As I climbed Nicole's front steps I knew what I had to do. I had to take control of the situation before it spun any farther out of my grasp. I had to break things off with Nicole and give myself a real chance with Jill. Right away.

"Hi, Craig," a cheerful voice greeted me.

Startled, I glanced up quickly. Nicole was

waiting for me on the screened porch. I'd been so deep in thought that I hadn't even seen her.

"Oh, um, hi," I said.

She gave me a small smile as she walked down to meet me, then linked her arm through mine. "Penny for your thoughts," she said lightly. "Looks like they might be interesting."

"Huh?" Her sudden appearance had taken me completely off guard. I hadn't had time to formulate a plan, to figure out how to break it to her. "Oh, I mean, no. Not really."

She gave my arm a light squeeze. "Okay," she said. "Why don't we head over to Lenape Avenue and get something to eat? Oh, and remind me to show you the flyer I picked up about Full Moon Fever. It sounds like a lot of fun. I can't wait till Monday."

I watched her as she chatted on, steering me slowly down the block toward the center of town. She looked perfect, as usual. And she seemed so happy to see me. My resolve was wavering already. Could I really do this to her? *Should* I?

My mind just didn't seem to be working right these days. That made me worry. Had my decision to ditch Nicole been too hasty? Or was I just looking for excuses because I was a complete and utter wimp?

I didn't know. But suddenly I knew I just didn't have the energy to deal with this that night. Besides, I *had* promised to take her to Full Moon Fever on Monday, and she was obviously looking forward to it. It wouldn't be right to strand her without a date at practically the last minute.

What difference would a few days make? It never hurt to be cautious. If things went well with Jill the next day, then I would know for sure. And after Full Moon Fever, I would sit down with Nicole and explain things to her calmly and rationally. In the meantime I would do my best to enjoy hanging out with her.

Even if all I could think about was being with Jill.

The next day I got permission from my boss, Mrs. Mackin, to leave the candy store a little early. As I said good-bye to her my cheeks flushed with embarrassment, thinking about how I'd told Jill that I was having dinner with her the night before. I just hoped that Jill would never ask her about it.

I hurried down the boardwalk to the gourmet food shop I'd noticed the day before, feeling my stomach clench with anxiety. When Jill and I had made plans, I'd insisted on taking care of the picnic myself. Now I was wondering if that had been the smartest thing to do. It wasn't as if I had a lot of experience planning romantic picnics for two. But maybe that was just my general nervousness talking. I couldn't wait to see Jill. I wanted everything to be absolutely perfect.

Inside the shop, I picked up a wire basket and looked around. I wasn't sure what kind of food Jill liked other than pizza. I decided to play it safe by bringing as wide a selection as possible. I selected pieces of fruit, cheese and crackers, Greek olives, French bread, and some freshly baked cookies. At the deli counter I ordered sliced ham and smoked turkey. I even remembered to pick up some plastic flatware and napkins. As I headed for the register, I spotted a display of gourmet doggy biscuits. Jill had mentioned bringing Romeo, so I tossed a bag of the treats into the basket. I figured the best way to a girl's heart might be through her dog.

As I pulled out some money to pay for the food, I noticed my hands were shaking a little. I wasn't sure if it was from anticipation or just sick, pathetic fear. I was still worried about my encounter with Jill on the street the day before. Had she suspected something funny was going on?

No question about it, I definitely wasn't cut out to be a Casanova, romancing more than one girl at a time. I was starting to think that not breaking up with Nicole the previous day had been a big mistake. There wasn't much I could do about it now. I grabbed the bag of food and left the store, trying to push the whole topic out of my mind.

Jill was waiting for me on a bench at the end of Lenape Avenue, just as we had arranged. I almost dropped the bag of food when I saw her. She looked more amazing than ever. That day she was wearing a pair of shorts and a loose white shirt, which fluttered unbuttoned over a floral-patterned bikini. She looked more beautiful, more vibrant, more *there* than any girl I had ever known or imagined.

Suddenly I didn't have to work to forget about Nicole. With Jill standing in front of me, I couldn't think about anything but Jill.

"Hi, Craig," she said. Romeo had been sitting under the bench at her feet. He leaped forward and barked at me happily.

"How's it going?" I could feel a goofy grin threatening to take over my face, and I bent over to pet Romeo for a moment to hide it. Goofy grins weren't usually my style. Then again, a lot of the things I thought and felt and did around this girl weren't my style. I should be getting used to it. "Hey there, boy," I said, ruffling the little dog's fur.

Jill picked up a large straw tote bag that was lying on the bench. She set it on the ground, then whistled for Romeo. "Come on, boy," she said. "Inside." The dog obediently raced over and hopped into the bag. Jill picked it up and grinned at me. "He's not supposed to be on the beach," she said, looking sly. "But as long as his paws don't actually touch the sand, nobody can really accuse him of breaking the rules, right?"

"Right," I agreed happily, that goofy grin threatening to break out again.

We stepped down onto the beach. It was crowded with sunbathers and kids playing and running around. Every inch of sand seemed to be taken up by a beach towel, a sun umbrella, or a lopsided sand castle. The hot summer sun was beating down and I was starting to sweat, though I wouldn't swear that the sun was completely responsible for that. Jill had just shrugged off her shirt and tucked it over the top of the bag to hide Romeo.

A brown-haired guy in a Johns Hopkins T-shirt was walking around and passing out fliers. He handed one to me. It was an advertisement for Full Moon Fever.

Jill peered over my shoulder. "Have you heard about that yet?" she asked me. "You should go— it's a real Lenape Beach tradition. Lots of fun."

"Um, yeah, I'll probably check it out." I nervously stuffed the flier into the bag I was holding. I was going with Nicole to Full Moon Fever— although right now that seemed like a big mistake—and I had to change the subject fast. "So, where do you want to sit down?" I asked.

"Let's go down this way." She tilted her head down the beach to the south. "I know where we can get a spot to ourselves."

"Lead the way." I shifted the big bag of food to my other arm so I wouldn't bump her with it.

She kicked off her sandals and carried them in her free hand as she headed for the moist sand along the water's edge. I quickly pulled off my sneakers and followed. The surf rushed up and swirled around our feet as we headed down.

I didn't want to let another awkward silence get started and ruin the happy, lighthearted feeling we had going. I tried to think of a conversation starter. "So, how was your parents' party?" I asked. "I hope you didn't miss too much of it."

Jill bent down to pick up a shell before she

answered. "Nope," she said, turning and flipping the shell into the waves. "I had a great time. The party was a huge success. And the band was fantastic. Mom and Dad danced until they collapsed."

"Cool," I said.

Suddenly the straw bag Jill was carrying started to wiggle wildly. A second later Romeo's head popped out from beneath the shirt and he let out a bark.

"Shhh!" Jill hissed frantically at him. She wrapped both arms around the bag and tried to shove the dog's head back in.

But Romeo wouldn't keep quiet. He stared at me and barked again. Then his tongue flopped out of his mouth and he panted eagerly, giving me a big doggy grin. That made me laugh, but Jill looked worried.

"Quiet, Romeo!" she whispered. "Naughty boy! Do you want to get us kicked off the beach?"

I noticed several people nearby looking around, puzzled. They were trying to figure out where the barking was coming from.

Romeo let out another yip. Jill glanced from the dog to me. "You know what?" she said. "Call me crazy, but I have an idea. Here, let's switch."

She held out the straw bag. I grabbed it, and Romeo whined with happiness and wiggled around like crazy. But when I gently pushed his head down, he settled calmly into the bottom of the bag.

"Hey, I guess he likes me," I said. I couldn't help sounding happy about it. I was pretty picky about girls and friends and just about everything else, but I was a sucker for anything with four legs and a wagging tail.

Jill laughed and reached for the grocery bag, which was still balanced in the crook of my other arm. "He's got good taste."

I was so busy peering into the straw bag to make sure Romeo was comfortable that it took a few seconds to realize that she'd just complimented me. My face turned red and I tried to think of something to say in response. But I'd missed the moment. Jill was already a few steps ahead, poking at something in the sand with her toe. I hurried to catch up, feeling annoyed with myself. When I reached her side I took a deep breath, forcing myself to chill. Getting uptight wasn't going to help me. Jill didn't look upset that I hadn't said anything. I had to relax and go with the flow.

We walked for a few minutes in silence after that. This time it wasn't like the awkward silences before. We were both just enjoying the beach, the sun, the cool water lapping at our toes. I didn't feel any pressure to say something clever or even to try to get a conversation started. Even hanging out with my friends back home wasn't this easy and relaxed.

The farther down the beach we walked, the less crowded it was. I looked across the sand and saw that the boardwalk had ended. The dunes were higher too, and dotted with patches of rough beach grass. Only a few people were strolling or sunbathing on the beach.

"Just a little farther," Jill said. "Up by the lagoon there probably won't be anyone at all."

She was right. We reached a spot where the beach was the only thing separating the sea from the glassy surface of a large, still lake. A few people were still in sight behind us, but not many. Jill left the waterline and led the way inland. I followed, clambering over the rolling dunes, the sun-warmed sand burning the bottoms of my feet.

When we reached the other side of the dunes, I looked around in surprise. In front of me was our own private beach. It was really just a spot in the sand about a dozen yards across. But it was hidden behind the dunes on one side and by a thick, high mass of sea grass on the other. The sea lay to the left, and the lake to the right. The only signs of civilization were the houses on the far side of the lake and a couple of boats out beyond the ocean breakers.

Jill stopped and glanced back shyly over one tanned shoulder. "I hope this is okay," she said. "It's where my friends and I come when we want to get away from all the people."

I couldn't answer for a second. I had a sudden, completely irrational feeling that if I spoke, this whole incredible scene would vanish like a soap bubble that's just been popped. I'd heard the words "too good to be true" but until now hadn't fully understood what they meant.

"It's amazing," I said at last. I gently lowered the straw bag to the sand, and Romeo hopped out and shook himself. Then he trotted around, sniffing at the sand.

"I'm glad you like it." Jill's eyes locked on mine and for a breathless moment we just stared at each other. *Into* each other.

She broke away first, turning to glance at her dog. "Stay, Romeo," she said firmly. "No playing in the water right now." She turned back and smiled at me. But the magical moment had passed. Her eyes were now unreadable. "He loves chasing waves." She set the food bag down on the sand, then pulled a beach blanket out of the bottom of her straw tote and shook it out. "You'll have to excuse the dog hair," she said apologetically.

I was still feeling slightly dazed from the intense look we had shared. But she was acting normal now, so I forced myself to do the same. I didn't want her to think I was some kind of lovesick nerd. Even if I was. "No problem," I said lightly. "It's my favorite part of any meal."

Jill began to take the food out of the bag and set it on the blanket. I reached over to help. We both grabbed for the bag of grapes at the same time, and her hand brushed mine. Her skin felt soft and warm, and I had the almost uncontrollable urge to slide my hand up her arm to see if her bare shoulders felt just as good.

I wondered if she noticed my face turning red as I quickly pulled my hand away. If she did, she didn't show it. She just oohed and aahed over the food I'd picked out, approving my choices.

When we reached the bottom of the bag, she picked it up and peered inside. "What?" I asked, ripping open one of the boxes of crackers. "That's everything."

"Um, Craig?" She sounded amused. "It was really great of you to get all this food. Was I supposed to bring the drinks?"

Oh, no! I'd brought all this salty food, but I hadn't even thought about bringing anything to drink! What did I expect us to do, guzzle down seawater?

"Oh, man!" I mumbled.

Jill giggled. "Don't panic." She jumped to her feet. "Watch Romeo for a sec, okay? I'll be right back." Before I could say a word, she took off over the dunes.

I lay down heavily on the sand, wondering if this was her way of ditching me. Romeo wandered over and bumped me with his cold, wet nose. My hand reached out automatically to scratch him behind the ears, and I felt myself relax slightly. She wouldn't have left her dog if she wasn't planning to come back.

"Get a grip," I whispered to myself. Romeo padded off again and I looked around. The least I could do was set up the food here.

I didn't even hear Jill coming a few minutes later as I carefully stuck a plastic knife into the jar of brown mustard I'd bought.

"Oh, Craig!" she exclaimed. "It looks great!"

I smiled. Those few little words were enough to

make up for all my humiliation. Usually when I got down on myself about something, nothing anybody said could make me feel better. But Jill seemed so sincere. So caring.

And I had to admit the spread *was* pretty impressive. I'd unwrapped and arranged all the food on the blanket. I'd set out the napkins, weighing them down with a small piece of driftwood. I'd picked up some shells too and formed a sort of abstract sculpture with them in the middle of the blanket, then stuck a few wildflowers into the top of it—that was a pretty nice touch.

Jill was carrying a six-pack of soda in one hand and a big bottle of water in the other. She set them down by the food.

"Where'd you get that stuff?" We were a good fifteen-minute walk from Lenape Avenue.

She shrugged. "It's the advantage of being a local," she explained. "My friend Donna lives a few blocks from here. Her mom let me raid their refrigerator."

"Oh." For a second I felt embarrassed again. If I'd been on the ball, Jill wouldn't have had to go rooting around in someone else's kitchen. But she didn't seem to mind, so I let it go.

Jill dropped to the sand at the edge of the blanket and started eagerly helping herself to the food. Before long she'd made herself a sandwich that had to be a good six inches high, maybe more. She crammed just about every ingredient I'd brought between those two pieces of bread. It looked good, so I decided to follow her example. I was glad to see that she didn't seem to be one of those girls who's always on a diet. It made things a lot more comfortable to know that we were both enjoying the meal.

And I *was* enjoying it—a lot. As we ate I couldn't imagine why I'd ever had trouble talking to her. All of a sudden there was so much to talk about that I felt as though we could never cover it all. We started off on safe ground, talking about dogs. But the conversation soon moved on to other things. School. Friends. Sports. Movies.

The only thing I really didn't want to talk about was my parents. I prayed that she wouldn't ask about them. Luckily, she didn't. And I was careful not to bring up the topic by mentioning her own family.

Before I knew it, the food was gone and Romeo had fallen asleep in the shade of the sea grass. I had no idea what time it was, and I didn't care. I'd never had a day like this before. I'd never known anyone like Jill before.

"Wow," Jill said, leaning back against the slope of the dune and closing her eyes. "I'm totally stuffed. That was great."

I grinned at her and then took another swig of my soda. That's when it happened. I should have seen it coming.

Braaaap!

The burp erupted out of me like a volcano. There was no way I could hold it in. No way I could stop it.

Jill's eyes flew open. She stared at me in surprise.

My face was flaming. "I—I—" I was totally humiliated. "I'm sorry," I said. "I mean, excuse me."

So much for our perfect date. Why did I have to be such a pig? I was surprised she wasn't running off in horror over the dunes already.

She didn't run. She didn't even look horrified. In fact, she started to laugh. She laughed so hard she couldn't speak. I wasn't sure how to react for a moment. But all of a sudden I realized how funny the situation really was. How ridiculous I was to get so upset about something so stupid and meaningless. I started to laugh too.

"Hey, what's going on?" I demanded jokingly. "Nobody laughs at Craig Miller and gets away with it!" I tossed a leftover pretzel at her.

"Oh, yeah?" Her eyes were mischievous. She grabbed the water bottle and doused my shirt with the contents.

The water was still cool from the refrigerator. I jumped up. "You'll pay for that, Gersten," I threatened. I lunged at her with a handful of sand, feeling reckless and playful. In other words, totally unlike my usual self.

She leaped away, shrieking with laughter. Romeo woke up and started barking and jumping around our feet, trying to join us as we chased each other all over our little private beach. By the time we stopped, too hot and exhausted to run anymore, we were both covered in sand.

"Whew!" Jill exclaimed, brushing a strand of

hair out of her eyes. "You win. Let's call a truce and go cool off."

"It's a deal," I agreed, still grinning. I had never just goofed around with a girl like that before. It was different. More like hanging out with a buddy than being on a date.

But Jill definitely didn't look like any buddy I'd ever known as she casually unzipped her shorts and slipped them off, leaving her in just her flowered bikini. I gulped and tried not to stare as she brushed sand off her body and headed down toward the ocean. Romeo had collapsed, panting, in the shade of the dunes.

My T-shirt was sticking to me, so I peeled it off. Then I followed Jill. A new feeling came over me, nearly bowling me over. It was a feeling of boundless joy and freedom and—okay, I'll admit it—downright giddiness. I didn't know where it had come from. Maybe from all that laughter and goofing around. Or maybe from Jill—after all, she was so full of life that it practically burst out of her. Why shouldn't some of that spirit rub off on me? I raced forward and grabbed her around the waist, spinning her around and around.

"Hey!" she cried. But she didn't really sound upset. "What do you think you're doing, you big lug?"

"Just helping you rinse off." I took a few more steps forward and dumped her in the water. She laughed and chased after me, trying to splash me.

We played around in the surf for a while. Then we staggered back up the beach and collapsed on the blanket. Jill still had a playful look in her eyes, though. As I leaned back to relax, she squeezed the water out of her hair . . . directly over me.

That did it. That put me right over the edge. I couldn't kid myself anymore about what was happening here. I had fallen for this girl. Totally and completely. It didn't make sense. I wasn't sure I wanted it to happen. But I was powerless to stop it.

I looked into her dancing ocean-colored eyes as she stretched out on the blanket beside me. She wasn't what the rational part of me would have chosen. Not in a million years. But maybe, just maybe, my rational side had gotten a little too dominant. Maybe Jill was exactly what I needed. She was definitely what I wanted.

I continued to ponder that for the next few minutes. The giddy mood had passed, and we were both just resting quietly in the sun. I wondered if Jill was having any of the same thoughts that I was.

I sat up and looked down at her. Her eyes were closed. She looked incredibly peaceful. And irresistibly beautiful. She must have sensed my gaze, because at that moment her eyes opened. She smiled up at me, then let them fall shut again.

"This is nice, isn't it?" she murmured.

That was the understatement of the year. "Absolutely," I replied. My voice sounded oddly husky in my own ears. I cleared my throat and quickly tried to think of something to say. Something innocuous, so she wouldn't see how emotional I was getting. Something wholesome and innocent, to take my mind off my sudden burning need to touch her. "Um, so you haven't talked about your family much," I said, trying to sound casual. "What are your parents like? What do they do?"

Too late I realized my mistake. Why had I brought up the subject of families? After we talked about hers, there was only one natural next step—to talk about mine. Exactly what I'd been hoping to avoid.

Still, maybe it was for the best. My family mess wasn't going away anytime soon, and if I was serious about Jill, I couldn't avoid the topic forever. It might be better to get it out in the open. Let her know what she was letting herself in for. See if she could handle it.

Several seconds passed and Jill was still silent. I wondered if she'd heard me. Then she finally spoke. "Oh, you know," she said without opening her eyes. "They're just parents. Mom's an elementary-school principal. My dad's a lawyer."

It was just what I might have expected. All-American jobs for an all-American family. "Cool," I said, my stomach tightening. Suddenly I didn't want to hear any more about Jill's parents. If I did, I might lose my nerve and be unable to admit the truth about my own family. "Um, you're lucky, I guess," I said. "I wish my parents had jobs like that."

I was doing my best to sound normal. But I guess it didn't work. She opened her eyes quickly and sat up. "What do you mean?" She looked concerned.

I took a deep breath. *Here goes.* "Well, everybody always tells me how serious and responsible I am," I explained. "But I have to be that way. To make up for them."

"Your parents?" she asked.

I nodded. "Mom and Dad are not what you'd call reliable." My voice came out sounding more bitter than I'd meant it to. "They came to Washington years ago to try to change the world. For some reason, they thought they could do that by being vegetarians and never holding down a real job." I sighed and stared down at the sand. "I'm probably being too hard on them. I admire their ideals, I guess. At least they've never compromised about what they believe in."

Jill was listening closely, her eyes never leaving my face. But she didn't interrupt. She just nodded, waiting for me to continue.

"They've had all kinds of crazy jobs over the years," I went on. "Then about five years ago they opened their own business. A macrobiotic food store. It did decently for a while. But they told me a couple of weeks ago that it's going bankrupt. And of course they have no savings."

"Oh, no," Jill said softly. "What are they going to do?"

I glanced at her. She was sitting with her arms wrapped around her knees, still watching my face intently, still looking concerned. I knew her sympathy and understanding weren't going to fix anything, but for some reason it made me feel a tiny bit better.

I shrugged. "They'll think of something. They always do." That was true. When I'd left for Lenape Beach, my parents were already talking to some friends about opening up some kind of nonprofit crisis center. That sort of thing wasn't going to pay my tuition at Georgetown, but at least it would be enough for them to get by.

"What about you?" Jill asked. "Are you worried about paying for college?"

"Definitely." I sighed. "The hardest thing is, I'm not sure they even understand why I'm so worked up about this."

Jill nodded. "Sometimes it's hard to remember that your parents are whole separate people, with their own ways of looking at everything. Especially when the things they do—the things they say they *have* to do to be happy—affect you."

I nodded, impressed by her perception. "That's true," I said. I paused for a moment, thinking about her comment. "But what do you know about that? Your family sounds cool."

Jill shrugged and looked down, her slender fingers toying with the edge of the beach blanket. "Oh, we're not so perfect," she said quietly. "My dad and I don't always get along so well."

The pain was evident in her eyes. "Do you want to talk about it?" I asked softly.

She shook her head and blinked hard. "No, forget it," she said. "There's not much to talk about anyway. It's just a personality clash. We don't believe in the same things, you know?"

"Sounds familiar," I said ruefully. "My brother and I have the same problem."

She seemed grateful for the shift in the conversation. "Well, we can't choose our own families, right?" she said. "Have you ever tried to talk to your brother about this money stuff?"

I snorted. "Nah. He's more like my parents that way—he takes things as they come and doesn't worry about them much. He probably wouldn't even care if he had to drop out of school. My parents practically had to beg him to go in the first place."

"Oh." Jill thought for a second, her eyes dark and serious. "Well, you're smart, right? Maybe you can get a scholarship."

"Maybe. But scholarships only cover so much. And my brother's going to be a sophomore this fall, so there will be two of us in school at the same time. . . ." My voice drifted off. There was no good solution. I'd been over it and over it in my head. As hard as I worked and as motivated as I was, I still might not be able to swing the college of my choice. Or any decent college at all.

It was all so hopeless. To my intense humiliation, I felt a prickling sensation behind my eyelids. Oh, no. Was I going to start crying on top of everything else? Jill would really be impressed with my manliness then.

Luckily she didn't seem to notice. "This can all be so hard sometimes," she said slowly, gazing out toward the waves. "So complicated."

I stared at her, amazed again at how well she understood. I couldn't believe we were actually having this discussion. I hadn't even talked about this stuff with my friends. "You're right," I said. "It *is* complicated. There's nobody to tell you if you're doing things right. Nobody who even wants to understand what you're trying to do."

She turned toward me and gave me a small, sweet, almost sad smile. "Almost nobody," she said.

What happened next felt completely natural. She scooted a little closer to me on the sand. Her arms reached out. I leaned forward. We hugged.

This wasn't like the hug back at the pizza place that first night. This was more like being wrapped in pure comfort. Pure understanding.

We stayed like that for a moment, just holding each other. Then it started to change. My heart started pounding a little faster. I suddenly forgot all about my parents and their problems and became very aware of Jill's body pressed against mine. I became aware of her scent, warmed now by the heat of the sun and flavored with the sharp saltiness of the sea. A strand of her blond hair was caught by a slight breeze and tickled my nose.

I loosened my hold and took her by the shoulders. I moved back just a little. Her head came up off my shoulder, and she looked at me with a question in her eyes.

This time I didn't miss the cue. I closed my eyes and leaned forward.

The kiss was amazing. Electric. Like nothing I had felt before. I lost myself in the moment and felt that there was nothing on earth except the pounding of the waves in my ears and the feel of her soft, warm lips on mine.

Nine

Jill

THE KISS WAS incredible. Like something in a dream, where even as you're dreaming you know it's just too astonishingly amazing to be happening for real. I had no idea how long it lasted. It seemed to go on forever.

Forever. Uh-oh. Suddenly cold reality broke in. What time was it anyway? I'd been having such a strange, topsy-turvy, wonderful, confusing time with Craig, I'd forgotten everything else. Even my date with Jasper. Whom I was probably supposed to meet any second now.

I pulled out of the kiss, trying to gather my wits and figure out how to make my escape without ruining the special time we'd had. When I opened my eyes and saw Craig's face so close to mine, I almost lost my resolve to leave. "That was nice," I whispered.

"Uh-huh." He leaned forward to kiss me again.

This time I forced myself to pull away after just a few seconds. It was one of the hardest things I'd ever done. But I couldn't just ditch my date with Jasper, no matter how tempting it was. I wasn't that kind of person. I'd made my plans, and I had to keep them—even though at the moment I thought I could be perfectly content to remain there on the sand, kissing Craig, for the rest of our lives.

I shook off that thought and smiled weakly. "I'm really sorry, Craig. I've got to get going."

He looked disappointed and a little confused. It made my heart ache. "Are you sure?" he murmured. He reached out and caressed my shoulder, a pleading expression on his face.

I bit my lip, resisting the strong urge to glance at my watch and the even stronger one to lean toward him and lose myself in that overpowering experience again. "I'm sorry," I repeated. I stood up, brushed the sand off my bikini, and pulled on my shorts. My legs felt wobbly. "I wish I could stay. But, um, I have a play rehearsal."

It was the only thing I could think of. I regretted the words as soon as they left my mouth. After our kiss, it felt horrible to lie to Craig. It was just a little white lie, but it felt dirty and wrong. It felt like cheating.

Where had *that* word come from? And why should a kiss change anything? Even if it was the most amazing kiss ever in the history of the world.

I felt light-headed and strange. Was this really me? I was acting so weird that day. First there had been that conversation about our families. I'd been on the verge of spilling my guts to him, which was unheard of. I had trouble discussing my family with my best friends. Why would I want to bring it up with a guy I'd only been out with twice? Now, to make things worse, one little kiss was making me question my whole philosophy of dating. Had I been out in the sun too long? Sure, Craig was cute, and smart, and funny, and nice, and thoughtful, and responsible, and . . . wait a minute. What was my point? I wasn't sure anymore. But I knew I had to figure it out quickly, before I lost my mind completely.

Craig still looked bummed as I tossed my stuff back into my bag. But he got to his knees and started cleaning up the remains of our lunch. "Just give me a sec and I'll walk you home," he said. "Or to your rehearsal, if you want."

"Oh, you don't have to do that," I said quickly. I was already going to be late meeting Jasper. "It's pretty far, and I'll have to hurry to get there on time. I'll just go myself."

He started to protest, and I stopped him with another kiss. I was careful to keep this one quick and light. But even still, my lips were tingling when I pulled away.

I had plenty of time to ponder my date with Craig as I sat listening to Jasper's band that night. I was sitting at a table off to one side of the stage, which was a raised section of the back deck at a place called the Rusty Anchor. The sun had set, and stars were beginning to twinkle over the bay, which lapped against the rocky shore a few dozen yards beyond the deck.

Jasper's band was called the Hoodlums. He was the lead singer. As I sat nursing a soda I wondered if the band had always been so awful. The music seemed to pound against my brain, making it hard to concentrate. And I wanted to concentrate. I really, really wanted to figure out what had been going on back there at the beach with Craig.

But my mind kept slipping away from the edges of the larger problem. It insisted on hovering around specific things, such as how utterly endearing he looked when he got that serious expression on his face. How thoughtful it had been of him to arrange such an elaborate, wonderful picnic. The way the corners of his eyes crinkled when he laughed.

I stirred the melting ice in my soda and sighed as the band finished one number and launched into another, even louder and less coherent than the last. I was pretty sure the drummer had started off on the wrong song, but I didn't think anyone in the audience noticed except me. To be honest, I didn't even think Jasper noticed. He was in his melodramatic brooding-rock-star mode, gripping the microphone in both hands and wailing out the lyrics with his eyes squeezed shut.

I had to admit it. I was touched that Craig had confided in me. I was glad it had happened. And then there was that kiss . . . I'd never been kissed like that before. I couldn't even remember what it had been like to kiss other guys.

This was getting scary. I sounded like somebody in a romance novel. Like someone who was— *gulp*—falling in love. That wasn't me. It couldn't be. I wasn't looking for a serious boyfriend. Craig was just another crush, like dozens of other guys I'd liked in the past. He had to be. Otherwise my whole world would have to change—*I* would have to change. And I wasn't sure I could face that.

I glanced up at the stage again. Jasper's face was coated with sweat. His long brown hair had come partly loose from its ponytail and was sticking to his forehead and neck. I tried to imagine him kissing me the way Craig had. For a second I almost thought I had it. I closed my eyes to savor the image, but as soon as I did Craig appeared in my mind, as if his picture were stamped on the backs of my eyelids. He looked much more real and solid than Jasper ever could. Much more handsome. More reliable. More incredible in every way . . .

My eyes flew open, and I let out the breath I'd been holding in a frustrated sigh. This was crazy. "Snap out of it," I muttered to myself.

"Talking to yourself again?" said someone behind me.

I looked around. It was Annabelle. "Hi," I said, raising my voice to make myself heard over a screeching guitar solo. I'd left a message for her at the theater telling her I'd be here. "How was rehearsal?"

She pulled out the chair beside mine and sat

down. "Exhausting," she replied. "Mr. Dinsdale actually decided to do a real run-through today."

"Just a run-through?" I said. "No standing on your head? No reading your parts in pig Latin?"

Annabelle shook her head, then lowered it onto her arms, which she'd crossed on the table. "Singing, dancing, the whole nine yards. What a workout." She gave me a tired smile. "Take my mind off my aching vocal cords. Tell me about your day with pizza boy."

I glanced at the stage. The guitar solo had ended, and Jasper was on his knees, screaming hoarsely into the microphone. "It was great."

I guess I sounded a little strange, because Annabelle sat up and gave me a funny look. "Oh?" she said. "Tell me more."

I shrugged. "It was no big deal, really," I said. "We had a picnic on the beach."

"And?" she prompted, grabbing my soda and taking a swig.

"And we goofed around. And talked." I couldn't help smiling as my mind drifted back over it all again. I almost forgot Annabelle was there. "He was really sweet. And kind of vulnerable, you know?"

Annabelle almost choked on the soda. "Huh?" she sputtered. "Am I so tired I'm hallucinating? Or did I actually hear you use the word *vulnerable* in a positive way?"

I started to protest, but I knew it wouldn't do any good. Annabelle had known me long enough to know when I was lying. "Well, okay," I relented. "I guess it *was* kind of weird. We talked about his family problems and stuff. And I didn't even mind. Not much anyway."

Annabelle cocked an eyebrow at me. "Really," she drawled. "That *is* weird. For you, I mean. It almost sounds like the kind of stuff a real couple would talk about."

"Give me a break," I said wearily. It was bad enough wondering if I was having some kind of schizophrenic breakdown without having to deal with this kind of grief from my relationship-crazy friends too. "It was just a date."

"Whatever," Annabelle said. "It's your life. For a second there it just sounded like you thought this guy was special. That's all." She signaled for the waitress and ordered herself a soda and some mozzarella sticks.

I thought about what she had said. Did I think Craig was special? I didn't have to think too long about that one. Of course I did.

But what did that mean? Once again I tried to think my way through it. Did it mean that I wanted something different this time? Something more exclusive—more permanent?

I shuddered at the thought. I couldn't believe I was thinking this way. *The horrible music must be going to my head,* I decided. Otherwise I would never consider giving up my fun-filled dating days for the boring life of the terminally committed. No matter what.

As the waitress hurried away to get Annabelle's order I tried to get my thoughts in some kind of order.

"You know," I said, "I think I've managed to hook up with a really great bunch of guys so far this summer. A totally interesting mix. Don't you think so?"

"Yeah, right," Annabelle said sardonically.

"I mean it," I said, gesturing toward the stage. "I mean, it's pretty cool to hang out with a guy who's the lead singer of a band."

"Yeah," Annabelle responded. "If the guy's Eddie Vedder. Not if he's some bad singer who thinks wearing a ponytail makes you a serious musician."

I wrinkled my nose. But I knew what she meant. I wasn't even sure that she was wrong—in this case at least. It wasn't as if Jasper could compare with someone like Craig.

Oops. That kind of thinking wasn't going to get me anywhere. "Okay, maybe Jasper isn't the best of the bunch," I admitted quickly. "I was starting to get a little tired of him myself. But what about Olaf?"

"What about him?" Annabelle shrugged. "He'll be going back to Norway in a few weeks and that will be it. And what good is a guy who doesn't even speak your language?"

I frowned. I hated to admit it, but once again there was something to what she'd said. Olaf was sweet, but when it came right down to it he and I really hadn't had much to talk about. And the language barrier couldn't be totally to blame. Craig could have been speaking Swahili earlier that afternoon and I still would have understood what he was all about.

Ugh! I had to stop this! "All right, then," I challenged Annabelle. "How about Roger? I had a nice time with him last night. And you've always said he was pretty cool."

"I didn't exactly say that," she corrected quickly. "I just said he was a good actor. And he's not bad-looking. What did you two end up doing last night anyway?"

It took me a second to recall anything about that date. It had been a pleasant enough evening. Roger was definitely more sophisticated than most of the guys I went out with. But somehow, nothing he'd said or done had really taken hold in my mind. I shrugged. "We just grabbed some dinner and went for a walk."

Annabelle didn't say anything for a moment. Onstage another song was ending. There was a pause while Jasper took a sip of water and wrung out his sweaty ponytail. Then he picked up the microphone again.

"Okay, gang," he shouted hoarsely at the audience. "We've got a very special song coming up next. It's one I just wrote for a special lady in my life, and I'd like to dedicate it to her." He looked toward my table. "Jill, baby, this one's for you!"

Jasper had written a song for me? How cool was that? Suddenly all my attention was on the stage for the first time that night. I barely had time to shoot Annabelle a triumphant look before the band ripped into the song. It started with a guitar riff that was actually sort of catchy. I grinned. Maybe I wasn't tired of Jasper after all. . . .

Then the lyrics started.

"Babe!" Jasper wailed. "You give me such a thrill. Oh, oh, ooooooh, Jill!"

I gulped and tried not to notice Annabelle's expression of disdain.

"Ooh, babe!" Jasper's eyes were squeezed shut with concentration. "Please say you will . . . be my baby, Jill!"

It was all downhill from there, although I was impressed that Jasper had managed to find so many rhymes for my name. *Still. Chill. Till.* And my personal favorite, *anthill.*

That turned out to be the grand finale of the show. Jasper jumped off the stage to scattered applause—including a few loud and, I strongly suspected, sarcastic whoops from Annabelle—and strutted toward me, looking very pleased with himself.

He grabbed me by the shoulders and leaned over to plant a big, sweaty kiss on my lips. I resisted the urge to dodge the mouth, but I couldn't stop myself from wiping my face afterward as he grinned and swung his leg over a free chair.

"Hey, babe," he said. "What'd you think of the new tune?"

"It was great," I lied. "I'm really flattered."

"Cool." Jasper leaned back in his chair, looking smug. He helped himself to one of Annabelle's mozzarella sticks.

I sighed and gave her an apologetic glance.

She just shrugged. "Yeah," she said. "Cool."

Ten

Craig

B Y THE TIME I got to work at the Sugar Shop on Sunday, I'd managed to confuse myself more than ever. I kept thinking about my incredible afternoon with Jill. And the weird way it had ended.

I knew she'd had to go to her play rehearsal. I respected that. But how could she have been thinking about something like a rehearsal during that kiss? If I had been the one with an appointment, there was no way I would have remembered it, even if it had been dinner at the White House. I tried not to let it bother me, but it did. Hadn't our kiss been as special for her as it had been for me?

I obsessed over that question as I measured out boxes of salt water taffy and homemade fudge. Why were girls always so hard to figure out?

Well, most girls. Nicole was the exception. She wasn't hard to figure out at all. She didn't play games. She didn't make me doubt my own feelings or wonder if I was going nuts. Had I let myself be blinded by my emotions or hormones or whatever and made the wrong choice? Maybe I'd been too quick to think that Jill was the one for me.

I noticed a smudge of chocolate on the counter and grabbed a rag to wipe it off. The store was almost empty. Mrs. Mackin was waiting on a family of tourists at the other end of the counter.

I was glad the place was quiet. I definitely needed more time to think about this. As far as Nicole knew, we were still going to Full Moon Fever together the next night. I had to decide what to do. Was I ready to cut her loose and take my chances with Jill?

"I thought we could start at the north end of the beach," Nicole said as we walked down her street Monday night under the swiftly darkening sky.

I still wasn't sure what I was planning to do that night. I felt paralyzed by my own doubts. About myself. About my crazy mixed-up feelings. About Jill.

Nicole had greeted me with a brief kiss, and now she took my hand as we walked. I didn't have the heart to pull away. "I heard that's where the courts are set up for the moonlight beach volleyball game," she went on. "There are supposed to be a bunch of food booths next to that, and then there's a temporary stage where some local band will be playing. We can dance if you want, or we can go on to see the shopping area—some of the local stores

112

are setting up stalls right on the beach. And at the far end they're holding a sand sculpture contest. I understand people have been working on their entries since sunup."

"Sounds like you got the whole scoop on this thing," I said. But for the first time, I felt slightly bothered by her no-nonsense approach. Didn't she ever just go with the flow?

The moon was rising as we crossed the boardwalk and stepped down onto the sand. The beach was already crowded with people of all ages. I could hear the band Nicole had mentioned starting to tune up a little ways down. Closer to us, several blaring boom boxes competed for attention. All around, people were smiling, eating, laughing, having a good time. The moonlight had a strange effect on the scene, almost as if we were all on a big stage lit with floodlights that made everything, from people to shadows to the sand itself, look just a little bit mysterious and out of kilter. Meanwhile, Nicole was discussing her class schedule for her first semester at Georgetown.

"Look," I said, interrupting a discussion about class size and teaching assistants. I pointed to the beach ahead of us, where a group of college-age kids had started a game of beach volleyball.

Nicole glanced over and nodded. "Looks like fun," she said briskly. "Come on, we should probably go get some food before it gets any more crowded. Otherwise we'll be stuck in long lines."

I followed as she marched off. It was a perfectly

sensible suggestion. So what if I wasn't really hungry yet?

I bought sodas, hot dogs, and cheese fries at one of the brightly colored tents in the food area. We ate as we walked over to check out the band. The members were still setting up on the square wooden stage that had been sunk into the sand about three quarters of the way up the beach toward the boardwalk.

"I guess they have to be careful where they put the stage," Nicole pointed out. "All those electric speakers and things could be a real danger this close to the water."

"Yeah," I said. "That would be shocking."

Okay, so it was a weak joke. But it sailed right over Nicole's head. She didn't even crack a smile.

We finished our food as we strolled along the stalls in the shopping area beyond the stage. Then we headed back to see if the band was ready to start. By this time the moon was directly overhead, the entire beach bathed in its silvery glow. The light reflected off Nicole's shiny brown hair and made her eyes and skin gleam.

I looked down at her. She had finally stopped talking. She was just glancing around, taking in the action-packed scene around us. The moonlight softened the angles in her face and made her look prettier than ever. So why wasn't I feeling anything for her?

She didn't seem to notice me staring at her. Her gaze had settled on the stage. "It looks like the band is ready to—" Her last words were swallowed up in an explosion of noise. The band had just launched into their first song.

I cringed. The music was terrible. But people were rushing toward the stage from every direction, transforming the sand between the stage and the ocean into a combination mosh pit and disco.

"Do you want to dance?" Nicole shouted into my ear. "Or should we sit down somewhere and listen?"

"Let's sit for a while," I yelled back. The makeshift dance floor didn't really look like my kind of scene. Under good circumstances I wasn't much of a dancer. With my distracted state of mind that night, I could be downright dangerous.

Nicole nudged me, pointing toward the wide strip of sand separating the musicians from the food tents. Someone had cleared away some sand while they were setting up the stage, creating a small sea of manmade dunes. A few people were already sitting in the hollows between these sand drifts, eating or just hanging out.

We found our own spot near the back of the stage. Since the speakers faced toward the ocean, it was a little quieter back there. I cleared away a couple of shells and a stray bottle cap. Nicole sat down with her back against a dune and patted the sand beside her.

I sat. She slid closer immediately, snuggling against me. "This is nice," she said with a contented sigh. "I'm so glad we came. Aren't you?"

"Sure," I said. But I was only half listening as I tried to get comfortable. Nicole's body didn't seem to fit right against mine. I held still for a second, but then I had to shift. Her shoulder was digging painfully into my side. To cover up what I was doing, I pretended I was moving so I could put my arm around her.

She turned her face toward mine. "It's been great getting to know you this past week," she said.

I couldn't answer for a second. I felt trapped. This was all wrong. I had to put a stop to it before it went any further.

Meanwhile the band had finished a song, and the lead singer, a short, skinny guy with a limp ponytail and a major attitude, was bellowing into the microphone.

"I hope you're all having a blast at Full Moon Fever!" he yelled. "We're the Hoodlums, and we're here to turn this into a major party!" With that, the band began another song.

I looked at Nicole, wondering how to tell her. She returned my gaze and smiled invitingly. This wasn't going to be easy. Trying to buy myself a few seconds, I glanced over her shoulder toward the stage, pretending to check out the band.

That was when I saw her. She was behind the stage, hurrying along across the moonlit sand near the boardwalk, all alone.

I knew that confident, bouncy walk, that long, shining hair. That face, already more familiar to me than my own. Jill!

116

My mind reeled. I don't know why—Jill had mentioned Full Moon Fever to me the other day. I shouldn't have been surprised that she was there. I guess I'd thought that since she'd lived in Lenape Beach for years, she might have had more than her fill of Full Moon Fever in the past. I was wrong.

Nicole reached up and started rubbing the back of my neck. "It's such a perfect night," she said softly. Then she leaned toward me, her lips parted slightly and a dreamy look on her face.

I dodged the kiss and jumped to my feet, turning my back to the boardwalk. I had to get out of there. Jill could come down this way at any moment. I couldn't let her see me with another girl! Whatever weirdness there had been at the end of our date, I was sure we could work it out. But not if she saw me with Nicole. That would make things too complicated. I had to find a more private spot and deal with this once and for all.

"Um, come on," I said to Nicole, speaking as quietly as I could while still being heard over the racket the band was making. I was afraid to look back and see if Jill was still in sight. "This music doesn't do much for me. And we never did get to see those sand sculptures." I grabbed her hand and dragged her to her feet, ignoring the look of amazement on her face. I felt terrible for what I was about to say to her. Mostly because I knew I should have said it days ago.

Eleven

Jill

I COULDN'T BELIEVE the Hoodlums were playing at Full Moon Fever. Why hadn't Jasper told me?

Annabelle and I had arrived a little late and headed straight for the shopping zone. I heard the band's first notes ring out from the speakers as Annabelle compared prices on woven bracelets.

Annabelle looked up abruptly. "Ugh," she said. "Is that who I think it is?"

I'd frozen at the first note and realized something at that moment. The old me would have welcomed the surprise of finding Jasper there. He would have been the perfect distraction from my own thoughts, which were mostly revolving around Craig. But now I didn't want to be distracted by someone like Jasper. Not that night, and not ever again. I would rather be alone than be with him.

I felt helpless to explain this to Annabelle. Fortunately, I didn't have to. One look at my anguished face told her as much as she needed to know for the moment—namely, that we had to avoid Jasper at all costs.

"Give me thirty seconds," she said briskly. "I'll head out through the dancers. If Jasper sees me, there's no way he'll turn around—he'll be too busy checking to see if you're with me. That should give you enough time to scoot around the back of the stage."

I shot her a grateful look that I hoped summed up exactly how much our many years of friendship and her unquestioning loyalty meant to me. "Gotcha," I said. "I'll meet you at the hoagie tent in five."

Annabelle disappeared into the dancing throngs. After a moment I saw Jasper craning his neck and stepping forward. He had spotted her. I darted around the shopping stalls to the narrow strip of empty sand between the stage and the boardwalk.

Taking a deep breath, I darted out from the crowd, my heart pounding fast.

I reached the other side safely. Jasper hadn't even turned his head. Soon I was able to dodge around the corner of one of the food tents.

I almost crashed into a couple heading my way. Fortunately, it was just Donna and Tim.

"Jill!" Donna exclaimed. "When did you get here? Where's Annabelle?" She had her arm wrapped around Tim's waist. The two of them were wearing matching Full Moon Fever baseball caps.

"Long story. What's with the nerdy hats?" I felt a little mean for saying it, but I couldn't help myself. It must have been all that adrenaline pounding in my veins. Fear will do that to you.

They just laughed and exchanged an amused glance. The moonlight made them look different than they usually did. Now that they were a couple, it was almost as if I didn't know them anymore. They had something new together that I could never be a part of.

"I've got to go," I muttered, pushing past them.

I headed for the hoagie tent. Before I could duck inside, someone grabbed my arm.

It was Annabelle. "Jill!" she hissed. "Red alert. Roger's here." She glanced around the crowded food area. "Somewhere."

My heart stopped. "Thanks for the warning," I said. I definitely didn't want to see him that night either. I was supposed to go out with him on Wednesday—I had agreed to that before my date with Craig—and I knew I'd have to deal with that somehow. But I couldn't handle it right then.

I grabbed Annabelle by the hand. "You know," I said quickly, "suddenly I just don't have much of an appetite. How about if we go watch the volleyball players for a while?"

"You got it." She led the way around the outskirts of the food area to the crowded sidelines of the volleyball courts.

We actually had a few minutes of peace. Don't get me wrong, it was a wild scene. The players were giving the game everything they had, and the spectators gathered around the court cheered them on enthusiastically. But we didn't see anyone we knew except Donna and Tim, who were sitting close together on the sand whispering into each other's ears as they watched the game. They didn't even notice us.

I had just started to relax when I spotted the trio emerging from a restaurant up on the boardwalk. The moonlight bounced off the tallest one's hair, making it look practically fluorescent. There was no mistaking that hair.

"Olaf!" I breathed.

"Huh?" Annabelle turned to look. She took in my horrified expression and grabbed my arm. "Come on. Let's go check out those bracelets again."

I trailed behind her numbly. I couldn't believe that I'd had the same reaction to Olaf as to all the others. I didn't want to hang out with Olaf anymore. I didn't want to hang out with Roger. Or with Jasper. Or with any of the other guys I'd met that summer. I had no desire to meet any of the cute strangers who surrounded me on every side. All I wanted was for them all to leave me alone.

Annabelle plowed down the beach, dragging me along, making a wide circuit around the food tents. Suddenly she came to an abrupt stop. "Uh-oh," she said. "I just realized. We're going to have to pass the stage again."

She was right. We couldn't stay on this side of the beach, with Roger at the food tents and Olaf near the volleyballers. I had no idea if the other side would be any safer—for all I knew, I could run into half a dozen of my old boyfriends over by the sand sculptures. In any case, I wouldn't be able to sneak behind the stage this time. The band's lead guitarist was back there. He seemed to be fixing a string.

I felt trapped and helpless. When had dating stopped being fun? When had being alone begun to seem like the best alternative?

Well, maybe not the best, a tiny voice inside of me piped in.

I ignored the voice. "Let's go wading in the ocean," I told Annabelle grimly.

She sighed and kicked off her shoes. "Is this how you treat your dates?" she complained.

"Come on," I ordered. "You stand on my left side so you're between me and the stage." I steered her down to the water's edge, hoping the dancing crowd hid us from Jasper.

We were about halfway past the stage when the band started a new song. The last song I wanted to hear right then. *My* song.

"Babe! You give me such a thrill. . . ."

I gritted my teeth. Every word seemed to bounce off the ocean waves and shoot back at me at double the volume. I hadn't thought anything could make me feel worse. But that did it.

By the time we got to the safety of the shopping stalls and the song ended, I was shaking. I wasn't going to be able to hold it together much longer. I needed time alone to think.

"Listen, Annabelle." I tried to sound more chipper than I felt. "This is getting ridiculous. You're not going to have any fun at all if we keep this up."

She shrugged. "Who cares," she said. "It's not like this is my first time at Full Moon Fever or anything. Do you want to go home and talk or something?"

"Thanks," I said, reaching over and squeezing her hand. She really was an amazing friend. But I needed to figure this one out for myself. "I'll be okay. Why don't you go find Donna and Tim?" I did my best to smile. "Or better yet, search for some cute new guy for yourself."

She opened her mouth as if to argue, then closed it again and nodded. "Okay," she said. "But come find me if you need me, all right?"

I watched her disappear into the crowd, then wandered toward the boardwalk, forcing my sluggish mind into gear.

I had to figure out why I couldn't get Craig out of my mind. And why I suddenly couldn't stand the company of any other guy.

The answer suddenly hit me—it was so simple that it was amazing I hadn't seen it before. I didn't want to be with those other guys. But it wasn't because I wanted to be alone.

It was because I wanted to be with Craig.

I shook my head in disbelief. It couldn't be. It had to be the moonlight. They said it could make people crazy. I wasn't ready to change my whole life for one guy. A *transient,* for Pete's sake. Was I?

I needed to go somewhere and make sense of this, try to understand what it could mean. How it would affect my life. But I didn't feel like going home. Most of the restaurants and stores on the boardwalk were still open despite the late hour, but there were too many people in them. I needed someplace private, where there was no chance of running into any of the guys I was trying to avoid.

My gaze fell on the sand sculptures a little farther down the beach. The sand sculpture contest was a big tradition in Lenape Beach, and as usual, people had put a lot of work into some of the entries. A couple of them were positively huge.

"Perfect," I murmured, heading that way. I could hide in the shadow of one of the sculptures and think for a while.

The theme of the contest was moonlight. I walked slowly past the first few sculptures, idly checking them out. It wasn't easy to see, since the real moon wasn't cooperating at the moment. It had drifted behind some heavy clouds, plunging the beach into near darkness. But most of the sculptures weren't exactly subtle, so I had no trouble making them out. There was a big telescope pointed at the sky. A giant chunk of Swiss cheese. A pack of howling wolves. And of course some clown had built a larger-than-life-size human form leaning over, with carefully sculpted pants dropped—mooning the moon.

Finally I came upon the largest entry of all. It was a life-size model of the Apollo lunar module. I decided it would make the ideal hiding place. If I sat behind it, the Swiss cheese would block me from view of the boardwalk. Total privacy.

I stepped around the module—and bit back a scream when I saw movement in the shadows. Then I saw what it was: a couple, sitting very close together on the sand. If I'd taken another few steps I could have stepped on them. But they were so wrapped up in each other that they hadn't even heard my footsteps. The guy was talking earnestly in a low tone, gripping both of the girl's hands in his own and gazing intently into her eyes. I moved back quickly to avoid interrupting. Luckily, they were so focused on their discussion that they hadn't noticed me, and I was glad. They looked so serious, so absorbed in each other. And then the guy leaned in and gave the girl a quick kiss on her lips.

The moon chose that moment to reappear from behind the clouds. As its silvery light illuminated the pair in front of me, I saw their faces clearly for the first time . . . and felt my heart swan-dive straight down to my knees. The female half of the couple was someone I'd never seen before—an attractive, slightly overgroomed girl about my age.

And the guy was Craig. *My* Craig.

I gasped and hurried around to the far side of the sand sculpture, even more shocked at my own thoughts than I had been at the sight of Craig kissing another girl. My heart was hammering so loudly in my chest that I was sure the whole town could hear it.

My Craig? Where had that come from?

But I finally knew the answer. Or rather, I accepted it. I leaned back weakly against the hard-packed sand of the sculpture as the full force of it hit me. Hadn't I really known it all along?

Craig was the guy for me. The real thing. My one and only.

There was just one problem: Now it was too late!

By the next afternoon my whole world had changed. I felt like a totally different person.

"I can't believe it," I moaned. I yanked on Romeo's leash to pull him away from a bulging garbage bag on the curb. My friends were keeping me company while I walked him. I'd already told them all about seeing Craig and my revelation. Now we were in the rehashing stage. I just couldn't seem to stop talking. "I didn't sleep a wink last night. I kept picturing that intense, emotional look on his face when he looked at that girl." I let out a miserable sigh. "It's a lost cause. I'm not going to go after some other girl's guy. I *never* do that." That was true. It was sort of a rule of mine and until now it had been an easy one to follow. After all, why fight over one tasty flounder when an even tastier bluefish was sure to come along right behind it?

Donna's eyes were huge and sympathetic. "Don't give up," she said for about the seventeenth time. "You never know what can happen. But if you want my advice, you should follow your heart."

"Is that your professional psychological opinion?" I joked weakly.

She smiled and shot Tim a sappy look. I wondered if anyone would ever give me a look like that. "Nope," she said. "That's just what I finally did. And I've never regretted it."

"You'd better be a little careful, though, Jill." Annabelle paused, balancing on one foot to dump a pebble out of her shoe. "It sounds like ol' pizza boy isn't the loyal, steady, one-woman type you thought he was."

"Way to state the obvious, Annabelle," I said sourly. We turned down Princequillo Street toward Lenape Avenue. Romeo was panting from the heat. It was one of those hot, sticky days when the whole world seems to move in slow motion. It was so hot that Donna and Tim weren't even touching for once.

"Annabelle's right," Tim put in quietly. "It sounds like this guy is more, um . . . well, more like you."

I stopped short. "Wow," I said. Romeo came to the end of his leash and stopped also, looking back in surprise. That got me moving again. But I was still in shock.

Everything I knew about Craig had led me to believe he was totally solid, reliable, honest—in other words, *not* the kind of guy to hang out with two different girls at once. On the other hand, I was pretty sure Craig might have thought the same about me. So what did that tell me?

I told my friends what I was thinking. Donna nodded solemnly as I finished.

"Does any of that change your mind about him?" she asked.

I wasn't sure. *Did* it change the way I felt? Was there really any future for a couple of hopeless flirts?

Finally I reached a decision. "I'm going to go for it," I declared.

Annabelle gave me a surprised look. In the humidity, her hair was curlier than ever. "Really?" she asked. "Doesn't it bother you that he's been going out with that girl behind your back?"

"What's good for the goose is good for the gander." They all rolled their eyes at the cliché, but I went on anyway. "If I can change my ways and decide he's the one for me, maybe I can get him to change his ways too." I chewed on my lower lip. "I just have to think of a plan. . . ."

"Um, Jill," Donna said. "Believe me, I'm all for your settling down with one guy. But I hope you're not planning to try to trick him into liking you. If you're serious about him, you need to change your style a little."

"What's wrong with my style?" I demanded. "It's always gotten me what I wanted before."

"You never wanted one particular guy before," Tim reminded me. "Donna's right. You have to be more open and honest with Craig. That's the only way you can know if it's going to work out."

Honest and open? The idea scared me. I wasn't

sure I could do it. But my friends were right. If I wanted a serious, mature relationship, I was going to have to start acting more serious and mature. Or at least try.

"Are you sure this relationship stuff is worth it?" I glanced around at the others.

"Absolutely," Donna said. "Once you get used to it, you'll wonder why you ever wasted all that time dating around."

I decided not to respond to that one. No matter what, I knew I would never regret the fun I'd had getting to know all those different guys. I had learned a lot from every one of them. That knowledge had helped me to finally understand what was happening to me.

I was in love.

"I'll do it." I glanced at my watch. Now that I'd made my decision, I couldn't wait to act on it. But I was going to have to wait, at least a little while. Half the transients on Mildred's staff had decided to call in sick this week, and I had promised to step in and work the dinner shift that night. "Rats," I said. "I've got to get moving, or Mildred will have a stroke. I'll track Craig down tomorrow and see if he'll meet me Thursday night to talk."

"Sounds like a plan," Annabelle said. "But why Thursday? Why not tomorrow night?"

I grinned guiltily. "Tomorrow night I have a date with Roger."

Donna and Tim exchanged an exasperated glance. Annabelle rolled her eyes.

"Hey," I protested. "You can't expect me to change completely overnight, right?" They didn't look convinced. I wasn't sure I was convinced myself. But I didn't want to hurt Roger's feelings. I would see him once more as planned, then let him down gently. It would be fine. "Just wait and see," I said. "If I'm lucky, by Saturday I'll be going to Annabelle's opening night with my new one-and-only boyfriend!"

Twelve

Craig

TUESDAY NIGHT I was still congratulating myself on finally doing the right thing by breaking it off with Nicole. She had seemed surprised and a little hurt when I'd explained that I just didn't want to get involved in anything serious with her, but she'd taken it in stride, as I could've predicted. We even shared a farewell kiss. I hadn't mentioned Jill at all. I knew if the situation were reversed, I wouldn't want to hear about the other guy.

Jill. I almost laughed out loud every time I thought about her. Now we were free to be together.

"Bro," Hewitt said, looking me over. "What's with you? You're acting like a total freak tonight. Did aliens abduct your brain or something?"

"Yeah," I shot back. "They finally figured out that yours didn't work."

I was out at a local pub having dinner with my

housemates. Normally that wasn't something I'd be eager to do, since Hewitt and Lara never let being out in public get in the way of their usual activities. But that night I was in such a happy mood that I would have done anything.

Luckily, at the moment Hewitt and Lara were keeping their hands and their lips to themselves. They were both sipping their drinks and eating peanuts. I leaned back in the seat next to Ed and closed my eyes.

I could hardly wait to see Jill again. I wanted to do something special for her to show how much I cared. Maybe that wasn't the most prudent course of action, but I couldn't help it. It just felt right.

I opened my eyes and found all three of my housemates staring at me curiously.

"Whoa." Hew actually looked slightly worried. "Really, dude. Is something going on with you?"

Lara nudged him in the ribs with her elbow. "I bet *I* know what he's thinking about." She smiled at me. "Nicole wouldn't tell me a thing about your date last night, but I'm sure it must have been fantastic. You two are so perfect for each other, and Full Moon Fever is always so romantic. When are you seeing her again?"

I was starting to feel more than a little uncomfortable. It hadn't even occurred to me to fill in my housemates about what I'd done. It wasn't any of their business. "I don't know," I mumbled. I grabbed a handful of peanuts and shoved them into my mouth, hoping Lara would take the hint.

"Come on," Lara wheedled. "You can tell us. We set you guys up, didn't we?"

I could tell she wasn't going to give up until she got some information. If she didn't get it from me, she'd get it from Nicole. "Actually, Nicole and I aren't seeing each other anymore," I said quickly. "I broke it off."

"What?" Hewitt looked amazed. "Are you out of your mind, bro? Nicole may be a little stuffy, but she's a babe!"

Lara punched him in the shoulder. "Shut up," she said. "She's not stuffy. Not everybody can be a big lazy goof like you, you know. She's a smart girl. Perfect for Craig."

Hewitt just shrugged and grinned, then took a swig of his drink. "Whatever."

The waiter brought our food and I hoped that would be the end of the discussion. But I had hardly sunk my teeth into my burger when Lara started in, describing how truly wonderful Nicole was and demanding to know what was going on with me and her. Or *not* going on, in this case.

Finally I'd had enough. She was giving me a headache. And Hew and Ed weren't being any help at all. They just listened and smirked while they ate.

"Okay, you want to know why I broke up with Nicole?" I blurted out at last. I felt my face turning bright red. "It's because I'm interested in someone else. Really interested."

That shut Lara up for a second. Hewitt leaned forward, looking interested. "Oh, yeah?" he said through a mouthful of cheddar burger. "You mean that other chick? The one from the pizza place?"

Lara shoved him again. "Don't say *chick*," she commanded. "It's sexist." She turned to me. "Is she the one? The pizza babe?"

I wanted to sink under the table. I should've realized they would figure it out. It wasn't as if I'd gone out with every girl in Lenape Beach.

"Her name's Jill," I muttered. "Jill Gersten."

Ed had been following the conversation impassively as he ate. But now he turned and stared at me. "Jill Gersten?" he said. "You're seeing *her?*"

"You know her?" I was surprised—Ed wasn't exactly a social butterfly.

Ed shrugged expressively. "Everybody knows her."

"What do you mean?" I asked cautiously. There was something about the way he was looking at me that I didn't like.

"I hung out with her a few times a couple of summers ago. It was no big deal." Ed paused. "It never is with her."

"What's that supposed to mean?" Lara asked.

"It means Jill likes to play the field," Ed said. "But she never lets things get too serious. She'll go out with a guy a few times, and then when she gets bored she lets him down easy."

"A serial dater," Lara said. "Wow." She cast me a sympathetic look. "And poor Craig's fallen for her."

"I haven't fallen for anyone," I said quickly. My

mind was racing. Could he really be talking about the same Jill I knew? The girl who had kissed me as though we were the only two people on earth? It was impossible.

On the other hand, in a way it made a weird kind of sense. It explained why she'd acted so oddly at the end of our date. As if our kiss hadn't really meant much.

"Don't sweat it, man," Ed told me without meeting my eyes. "You're not the first guy who's been slammed by that girl."

I sat back heavily in my seat. Jill wasn't interested in me. She went out with lots of guys. I was just one in a long parade of dates. I remembered the beefy guy from the pizza place. Whom would she enlist to ditch *me* when the time came?

I didn't know why I was surprised. Hadn't I predicted this from the very beginning? After all, she'd been playing games the first time we'd met. I should've known she was just toying with me. My brain could have told me that this girl was nothing but trouble. If I'd bothered to listen to it.

I glanced around the table. The others were eating quietly, pity in their eyes.

I reached a decision. My head was back in command and my heart could go jump in the ocean.

I sat up and reached for a french fry. "So, Lara," I said, "do you think Nicole would give me another chance?"

She smiled. "There's only one way to find out," she replied, digging into her shorts pocket and tossing me a quarter. "Give her a call."

Thirteen

Jill

ON WEDNESDAY AFTERNOON I peeked into the Sugar Shop and saw Craig standing behind the counter refilling a tray of taffy. I checked my reflection in the plate-glass window, then pasted a big smile on my face and went inside, feeling nervous. I'd been anxious and jittery for the past twenty-four hours. The night before at work I'd been such a basket case that Mildred had sent me home early. Was this really what being in love was about—sweaty palms and a constant knot in the pit of your stomach?

A little bell tinkled as the door swung shut behind me. "Hi, Craig," I said, feeling my fake smile melt into a real one as I looked at him.

He glanced up. His face remained neutral. "Hello, Jill."

I gulped. I'd expected a slightly more enthusiastic reaction. Had I misjudged things somehow? I couldn't let myself get sidetracked now. I plowed on. "I was just walking by and I saw you here, so I thought I'd stop in and say hi." The words came automatically, before I could stop them, even though it wasn't what I had planned to say at all. It wasn't the truth.

"Really?" Was it my imagination, or did his voice sound a little frosty? He'd already gone back to what he'd been doing. He wasn't even looking at me anymore. Maybe this was all a big mistake. Maybe that other girl meant even more to him than I'd imagined. Maybe I had no chance at all.

Before I could figure it out, the door opened and I heard a very familiar voice. "Jillie! What are you doing here?"

I turned around slowly. This was all I needed right now. "Hi, Mom," I said weakly. "Um, nothing much. I just stopped in to talk to a friend of mine."

My mother glanced at Craig and smiled. "Oh, hello." She stepped forward and extended her hand. "I'm Jill's mother."

"I'm Craig." Craig shook my mom's hand politely. "It's very nice to meet you," he said. "Jill has told me a lot about you."

"Oh, really?" My mom looked surprised.

Craig nodded and smiled. "I understand you had quite a party last weekend."

I froze. What on earth had made me come up with that stupid anniversary party in the first place? "Uh, that's right. Mom's a regular party animal.

Right, Mom?" I crossed my fingers and prayed that she wouldn't give me away.

"Sure, Jillie." She gave me a long, perplexed look. "If you say so." That was one thing you could always count on with my mother. She never asked too many questions.

"Don't you need to get going?" I asked my mom with a pleading look. I didn't want to drag this out any longer.

"Well, I *was* on my way to meet a friend," my mom said, confusion evident in her expression.

"All right then, bye," I said quickly. "I'll see you at home."

My mom opened the shop door and paused to give me one last puzzled glance. "Okay, honey," she said. "I'll see you later. It was nice meeting you, Craig."

"Same here, Mrs. Gersten," he replied.

I smiled uncomfortably at my mom before she walked outside. I'd explain it all to her later. Maybe. Right now I had other things to worry about.

Craig was looking at me oddly. "You didn't seem too happy to see her," he said. "I thought you two got along."

"Oh, we do," I assured him quickly. "But I didn't want her to be late. She's always running late. It's a bad habit."

I was starting to feel a little calmer. Okay, so my mom and Craig both thought I was acting like a nut. But I'd managed to avoid disaster back there, and that hadn't been easy.

I took a deep breath as Craig went back to work with the taffy. "So," I said. "Um, I was wondering . . ." How had I managed to ask him out that other time? The words had come so easily then. "Are you doing anything Thursday night? I mean, if you aren't, would you like to get together or something?"

Craig didn't look up. He just kept staring at that stupid taffy as he methodically stacked it on the tray. "I'm sorry," he said. "I can't make it on Thursday."

My heart seemed to drop into my stomach, and the air-conditioning in the store suddenly felt very cold. So this was what it felt like when your heart split in two. As if your insides were on fire and your outsides were going to spontaneously combust if you stood in the same spot for one more second. "Um, okay," I mumbled. "See you around."

I turned and fled before he could look up. Out on the boardwalk, I ignored the happy crowds and shoved my way in the direction of home. The rejection itself wasn't even the worst part. Much worse than that was the overwhelming sense of loss and despair that followed on its heels. The guy I wanted didn't want me. He didn't want me.

And there was nothing I could do about it.

Fourteen

Craig

ON THURSDAY EVENING I walked over to pick up Nicole. But I was thinking about Jill.

I still felt awful for turning her down. The vulnerable look in her eyes haunted me. It didn't help much to remind myself that I'd vowed to forget her. I'd wanted to keep things cool between us. I really did. But my resolve had started to slip the second she'd walked into the candy shop.

And then when her mother came in, Jill had suddenly seemed so nervous and jumpy in front of her. It was sort of cute—it made her seem more like a regular girl and less like the nonstop dating machine Ed had described.

I was almost to Nicole's. I slowed my pace. We were supposed to go out and get something to eat, and I knew what that meant. We would spend the whole evening discussing important things like schedules and grading curves and course loads.

Before we got into all that, I needed to sort out my thoughts.

Was I ready to give up on Jill and commit to Nicole? That would be the sensible choice. But I kept remembering how disappointed Jill had looked the previous day. Was there a chance—just maybe—that Jill could change her roaming ways to be with me?

I was probably kidding myself. But I knew it was nothing but dumb luck that I hadn't said yes to Jill the day before. It was only because she'd wanted to get together on a night when I already had plans with Nicole.

I stopped on Nicole's front steps. Should I cancel this date? Should I call Jill and see if she still wanted to get together? Or should I just let things be?

Before I could decide one way or the other, the door opened.

"Hi." Nicole looked flawless, as always. "What are you doing? I saw you standing out here."

"Oh!" I said. I couldn't put Nicole through another discussion. Or maybe I was a big wimp. "Uh, nothing. I thought I might be too early, that's all."

Nicole walked down the front steps. "Nope," she said. "You're right on time."

I was in no state of mind to take charge of our plans. Luckily, Nicole was ready to step in.

"I've been hearing good things about the Thursday night all-you-can-eat seafood special at one of the local restaurants," she said as she steered me down the street toward Lenape Avenue. "It's a place called Crabby Kate's."

"Sounds good," I said. I was now sure that this date was a big mistake. What had I been thinking, asking her out again in the first place? I guess I'd been so upset about what Ed had said about Jill, and then with Lara glaring at me across the table . . . I don't know, I guess I'd crumbled and somehow thought this would be a good idea. It definitely wasn't. There was only one thing I could do now—try to make it as painless as possible for both of us. "Lead the way."

When we arrived at the restaurant the hostess, a plump older woman, seated us near the middle of the room. "Your waitress will be with you in a jiff," she said, dropping a couple of menus in front of us.

Nicole opened her menu. "I think I already know what I want," she announced. "A big glass of grapefruit juice with lots of ice and the seafood feast."

I was about to respond when all of a sudden I was rendered completely speechless. A waitress was approaching our table. She was dressed in shorts, a T-shirt, and an apron with little blue crabs printed all over it. But it wasn't the outfit that caught my attention.

It was Jill. She recognized me at the same time that I recognized her. But she didn't say anything to acknowledge it. She just gave us a rather strained-looking smile and said, "Hello, my name is Jill. I'll be your waitress tonight."

I swallowed hard as I looked up at Jill. I was such

an idiot! Jill had told me that she waitressed at a beachside restaurant—why hadn't I thought of that when Nicole suggested we come here? Well, it was too late now.

Nicole didn't even glance up. She was still scanning the menu. "We're not ready to order yet," she said. "But you could bring me a grapefruit juice with lots of ice, please." She looked over at me. "You want anything?"

Jill was staring at the table. I was trying not to stare at her. She looked beautiful, as usual. I wanted to jump out of my seat right then, take her in my arms, and never let her go. How had I ever thought I could forget her and go on with my life?

"Craig?" Nicole prompted. She reached over and rubbed the back of my hand. "Wake up."

I remembered where I was. And who I was with. What was I thinking? It was obvious to anyone with half a brain that Nicole and I were there on a date. And it was equally obvious from the way she was acting that it wasn't our first. Any chance I might have had to make things right with Jill was gone. She'd never take me seriously now.

"Um, I'll just have water," I managed finally.

Jill nodded and hurried off. I watched her disappear through a doorway at the back of the room, my heart twisting painfully.

Nicole still had her face buried in the menu. "You know, I think I changed my mind," she said. "I might have the crab cakes instead of the special."

"That sounds good." A couple of crab cakes had

to be quicker to eat than the seafood special. And I wanted to get out of there as soon as humanly possible. "I'll have the same."

"Good." Nicole closed her menu and leaned back in her seat.

Jill returned, carrying a glass in each hand. "Here you go," she said, setting one glass in front of each of us.

Nicole looked down at hers and frowned. "This is water."

"Yes?" Jill asked uncertainly. I could tell that she was trying very hard not to meet my eyes. I didn't blame her. As humiliating as this was for me, it had to be twice as bad for her. After all, now she knew why I hadn't been free to see her.

Nicole sighed. "I ordered grapefruit juice. Extra ice."

"Oh!" Jill looked flustered. "Juice. That's right." She started to pick up Nicole's water glass.

"Leave it," Nicole said, stopping her. "I'll keep the water now that it's here. Just bring the juice too."

Jill nodded and started to turn away.

"Wait," Nicole said. Jill stopped and glanced back at her. "We're ready to order."

"Oh, okay." Jill's cheeks were bright pink. My heart ached with guilt. She reached in the pocket of her apron and eventually came up with a pad and a pencil. "We have a few specials tonight. Um . . ." She looked blank.

"Never mind." Nicole glanced at me and rolled

her eyes. "We already know what we want. We're both having the crab cakes."

"Okay." Jill made a note. "Um, that's crab cakes. For two." She still didn't meet my eyes. She didn't even look up from her pad.

"What a ditz," Nicole said quietly as Jill hurried away. "Anyway, what were we talking about? Oh, yes . . ."

The insult hurt as much as if it had been aimed at me. Who was Nicole to criticize Jill? She was doing her best under incredibly difficult circumstances. But I couldn't say anything. Not without making this whole situation even messier and more embarrassing for everyone.

Nicole didn't notice any of my internal struggle. She was off on another one-sided conversation about something or other. I think it was the impact of interest rates on her student loan. But I wasn't sure. I was too busy trying not to stare as Jill moved in and out of the kitchen and around the dining room waiting on other customers.

I felt terrible. This was an incredibly awkward position for both of us. Not to mention depressing. How had I ever thought I could be happy with Nicole? Or with anyone else? Jill was the one I wanted. The only one. I should have recognized that from the beginning. But like the idiot I was, I'd tried to talk myself out of it. I had used any excuse I could find: the way she looked, Nicole, and now Jill's dating habits, according to the word of one guy—a guy I didn't even know that well.

But none of that really mattered now. It was too late. I had spoiled things with Jill, and there was no way I could go on pretending with Nicole anymore. I'd gone from two girls to none in one fell swoop. All I wanted now was to end this miserable evening as soon as possible.

It was a while before Jill returned with our food, but she finally raced over with two plates. "Here are your crab cakes," she said breathlessly. She slid a plate in front of each of us and turned to depart.

"Wait." Nicole's sharp tone stopped Jill before she had taken more than two steps. "Aren't you forgetting something, miss?"

Jill was blushing furiously. "I'm sorry," she said. "Was there something else you wanted?"

Nicole sighed loudly. "Yes," she said, enunciating her words as carefully as if she were talking to a slow-witted toddler. "You never brought my juice."

"Oh, that's right," Jill said. "I'm so sorry. Let me just run and get it now."

"*Thank* you." Nicole shook her head as Jill rushed away. "Give me a break," she muttered. "It's not like this is brain surgery."

I wanted to come to Jill's defense. But I couldn't say a word without giving myself away. So I picked up my fork and poked at my food, keeping silent as Nicole continued to mutter about incompetent waitresses and the national job shortage. Or something along those lines.

Jill returned quickly with a single glass. She set it

down in front of Nicole. "There you go," she said. "Sorry for the delay. Now, will there be anything else?"

Nicole was staring at the glass. There was a look of disbelief on her face that made her sharp cheekbones stand out more than ever. "This is orange juice," she said evenly.

"Yes," Jill said, looking confused. Suddenly she gasped. "Oh, no! You ordered grapefruit juice, didn't you? I'm so sorry. . . ."

She reached for the glass at the same time that Nicole started to push it away. The glass teetered . . . and fell. Orange juice splashed across the table and into Nicole's lap.

"Aaah!" Nicole screamed. She jumped to her feet and grabbed for a napkin. "You clumsy idiot!" she said, dabbing at her skirt. "Can't you do anything right?"

Jill's greenish blue eyes were filling with tears. "I'm sorry," she whispered. "Here, let me help you."

She pulled a rag out of her pocket and reached toward Nicole's skirt. Nicole saw the splotch of red seafood sauce just in time and leaped backward. "Get away from me," she cried. "Just get lost."

That did it. Jill started crying for real. And that was all I could take.

"Shut up, Nicole," I snapped. "It's not that big a deal."

She stopped what she was doing and stared at me in shock. "What?"

I could see that she was about to start yelling again. I got up and grabbed her by the arm. "Come on. Let's step outside for a second." I dragged her toward the door before she could protest. In the small lobby area, I spotted a sign for the rest rooms. "Why don't you go clean yourself up?" I said. "I'll meet you outside in a minute."

"Fine," she said icily, scowling at me. "There's no way I want to eat in this stupid place now anyway." She strode off toward the ladies' room.

I hurried back inside. Jill was on her hands and knees, tears running down her cheeks as she dabbed at the wet spot where the orange juice had dripped onto the rug. The woman who had seated us was hovering over her, looking worried.

I took a deep breath and walked over to them. "Hi," I said to the older woman. "I'm sorry about that. Um, could I talk to Jill for a second?"

She looked me up and down, then nodded. "Jill," she said briskly, "I'll finish here. Take five, okay?"

Jill glanced up at me and gulped. Then she clambered slowly to her feet. "Craig?" she whispered. "I'm sorry."

"Is there someplace we can talk?" I asked. "I have a few things I want to say."

She looked nervous at that, but at least her tears had stopped. She sniffled, nodded, and led me back through the kitchen. A moment later we were standing in the alley behind the restaurant, surrounded by garbage cans and stacks of empty crates.

She started talking immediately. "I'm really sorry, Craig," she said. "I know your girlfriend thinks I'm a jerk, but I just—"

"She's not my girlfriend," I interrupted. "Uh, that's sort of what I wanted to talk to you about." I took a deep breath. There was no turning back now. And suddenly I knew I wouldn't turn back even if I could. I had to say this, no matter what response I got. "Jill, I don't care about that girl. I—I care about you."

The words hung between us for a second. She stared at me, looking confused. Then she started to smile. "Really?" she said. "I mean, that's great! I mean, I care about you too."

I felt a huge rush of emotion. It started as disbelief, then turned to relief for a second before melting into overwhelming joy. "Great!" I reached out and grabbed both her hands in mine. "Listen, Jill. I won't lie to you. I was seeing that girl the whole time I've known you. And I never had dinner with Mrs. Mackin—that was just a cover. I'm sorry, that was all a big mistake. You're the only one I want to be with."

"Me too," she said shyly. "I mean, you're the one I want to be with too. If you say she doesn't mean anything to you, I don't care about that other girl."

I waited for her to say something about seeing other guys. But she just smiled at me silently, looking happy. For a second I felt a nagging twinge of doubt. Was she still playing games? Or had Ed been exaggerating about her dating habits? Yeah, I decided now, he probably still had the hots for her himself and was jealous that I was seeing her. And maybe Jill had dated a few guys in summers past. But now she was with me. That was all that mattered.

I reached out and wiped a stray tear from her cheek. "Listen," I said, "I think it's time to put all this stuff behind us. Can I see you tomorrow night?"

"Tomorrow?" Jill repeated. "Um, that's Friday, right? I can't. I'm sorry. I have play rehearsal."

"Oh, right." I had forgotten about her play. "*My Fair Lady,* right? Well, that's okay. I can wait, I guess." I grinned at her. "How about Saturday afternoon? We can have another picnic if you want. That will give us a chance to really talk things out."

"That sounds perfect," she said. "I'll bring the drinks, okay?"

I felt a laugh of pure happiness bubbling up inside me. It didn't matter that Nicole was out front waiting for an explanation. I was almost looking forward to giving her one. I had a few choice words for her about her little tantrum. And breaking up with her—for good this time—was the last thing standing in the way between Jill and me. "It's a deal."

I took a step closer, put my arms around her waist, and pulled her close. Her eyes fluttered shut, and she tipped her head back. Our lips met.

That kiss told me everything I needed to know. I had finally done the right thing.

Fifteen

Jill

I SHOULD HAVE been ecstatic after my talk with Craig. Positively blissful. And at first I was. Finally I understood what my friends kept raving about—what it was like to be with one special person and wish it could go on forever. All the guys I'd dated in the past were suddenly a big blur. Why had I bothered? This was what I'd been looking for all along.

Then a few nagging little thoughts started intruding on my living daydream—memories of lies I'd told him and truths I hadn't. He'd given me the perfect opening to tell him about my dating history. But I'd been too afraid to do it. What would he think when he found out?

By the time I got off work the next afternoon I was a nervous wreck. I untied my apron and hurried out the back way. As I stepped outside I paused, looking around. My face felt warm as I remembered being there with Craig. Why had I lied to him about what I was doing that night? All I was supposed to do was go see Jasper's band. I could have canceled that. I'd *wanted* to cancel it. But I'd been so flustered that I'd simply gone on autopilot.

For a second I considered telling him the truth: That I wasn't playing Eliza Doolittle. That my parents hadn't had any big anniversary party. That I'd really been out with other guys all those times . . .

I couldn't do it. I could almost see the horrified look on his face. And I couldn't take any chances now that I'd finally found the guy of my dreams. As long as I vowed to be honest with him from this point forward, what harm was there in letting Craig go on believing a few little fibs?

I started for home, feeling slightly calmer. The phone was ringing when I let myself in the back door. "I'll get it!" I yelled.

"Thanks, Jillie!" my mother called from upstairs. There was no word from my brother. He didn't use the phone. When he wanted to communicate with one of his pasty-faced computer cronies, he used E-mail.

I grabbed the phone. "Hello?"

"Hi, Jill," a deep, warm voice replied. "It's me. Craig."

I sank down onto a nearby chair. Was this what romance novels meant when they said the heroine got weak in the knees? I didn't know, but I liked it.

"Hi," I said. "Are you at work?"

"Nope, I just got home," he replied. "Listen, I can't wait to see you again."

"Ditto," I said. "I'm really looking forward to tomorrow afternoon." I smiled as I pictured the two of us on the beach again. This time I wouldn't have to break up our kiss until it was time to leave for Annabelle's play.

My smile faded slightly at that thought. So much for taking my new boyfriend to opening night. I'd have to come up with another little white lie to explain what I was doing the next evening.

"Same here," Craig said. "But I just had a great idea." He paused and laughed softly. "Well, actually, it was my brother's girlfriend's idea. But I don't know why I didn't think of it myself. Why don't I come to your rehearsal and cheer you on?"

My mind went blank. Totally blank. A complete log jam. "Um . . . ," I said.

"Come on, you may as well give in." His voice was light and teasing. "I won't take no for an answer. I even called and got directions already. The Lagoon Dinner Theater, right?"

My mind suddenly clicked into gear again, rushing along at three times normal speed. I had to do something. I thought about telling him visitors weren't welcome at rehearsals. That had worked the previous week on Boring Bob. But it was too risky. For all I knew, Craig might have talked to Mr. Dinsdale himself. If he'd identified himself as a friend of mine, the director would have begged him to come, transient or not.

This was it. There was no way out. I had to tell Craig the truth. Now.

I cleared my throat. "Okay, cool," I said.

I felt like kicking myself. I was such a wuss!

"Great," Craig said. "This will be fun. See you there."

He hung up before I could say another word. I stared at the buzzing phone receiver in a panic. What was I going to do now? I'd missed my cue. My last good chance to be honest. Even if I called him back right now, I would end up looking like a real jerk.

So I called Annabelle instead. "Annabelle," I said as soon as she picked up. "I've got to ask you the biggest, most stupendous favor one friend ever asked another. . . ."

"You realize this is our final dress rehearsal, don't you?" Mr. Dinsdale said.

It was twenty minutes later. I had canceled my plans with Jasper, and Annabelle and I were in Mr. Dinsdale's tiny, cluttered office behind the stage at the dinner theater.

"We know," Annabelle told him. It had taken a lot of begging and pleading to convince her. But she'd never seen me this serious about a guy before, and she just couldn't resist. "But you said yourself that we were perfect at yesterday's run-through. And you're always saying that a good final dress rehearsal means a miserable opening night and vice versa, right?" She grinned. "Well, with Jill playing Eliza, I can safely guarantee you the worst dress rehearsal in history."

"Thanks a lot," I muttered. I gazed at the director

158

earnestly. "I won't be that bad, Mr. Dinsdale. You know I've watched about a thousand of your rehearsals. And I've seen the movie dozens of times. I know the whole show by heart." I gave him what I hoped was my most winning smile. "Think of it as an exercise for the other actors."

Mr. Dinsdale was silent for a long moment. He hadn't seemed particularly impressed when we'd told him the reason for my bizarre request, but he hadn't immediately said no either, which gave me hope. I crossed my fingers and held my breath, not daring to think past the next few seconds. I didn't know what I would do if he said no. I wasn't exactly sure what I'd do if he said yes either, but that was another story.

The director looked from me to Annabelle and back again, pursing his lips thoughtfully. "All right," he said suddenly. "We'll do it." He grinned and poked me in the shoulder. "I'll let the rest of the cast know. Girlie, we're gonna make you a star!"

I was so relieved that for about three and a half seconds I didn't have time to panic. Annabelle and I hurried out of the office into the backstage area. The heavy velvet curtain was down, and I peeked through them to see if Craig was there yet. He was sitting in the front row.

"Oh, God," I whispered. "He's talking to Roger!" What if Roger said something incriminating? I could practically hear it now. *Oh, you're here to see Jill? Lovely girl. Why, I gave her a big, fat, juicy kiss myself just the other night. . . .*

Annabelle shrugged. "There's nothing you can do about that now," she said crisply. "Come on, let's get you suited up."

She dragged me to the wardrobe room and helped me into her costume for the opening scene. Naturally, the bottom hem of the dress was about half a foot too long, and the sleeves came down to my knuckles. But it's amazing what an experienced actress such as Annabelle can do with a handful of safety pins.

Before I knew it, I was stepping onstage.

The orchestra struck up the opening notes. I felt incredibly nervous, and I knew it had nothing to do with stage fright. I didn't care how lousy I was, as long as Craig didn't suspect anything. Roger wouldn't give me away.

Between watching rehearsals, helping Annabelle learn her lines, and viewing the movie on video-tape, I had to have seen or heard Eliza's first scene in *My Fair Lady* at least seventeen hundred times. Despite that, my mind blanked out on at least half of my lines, and the other actors had to bail me out. It was sort of like a dream I'd had once where I got a job as a welder. It wasn't until I was hundreds of feet above the ground on some kind of beam, with all sorts of strange welding tools in my hands, that I realized I had absolutely no idea what I was doing.

Somehow I survived the scene. As the lights dimmed and the stagehands scurried about doing their business, I carefully peeked out of the wings at

Craig. I could barely see him in the front row of the darkened theater.

Annabelle stepped up beside me. "Brava," she whispered. "You're practically ready for Broadway."

I rolled my eyes. Only Annabelle could manage to sound sarcastic and supportive at the same time. "Gee, thanks," I replied. "Maybe I should head there now. At least it would get me out of town before I have to explain to Craig why they gave the lead in this play to someone who can't even carry a tune."

"Don't worry about it." Annabelle shrugged. "You'll think of something. You may not be tearing up the stage, but nobody can hold a candle to you when it comes to real-life acting."

I stared at her. My mind was clicking into high gear again.

What was I doing? Why was I putting myself through this?

At best I would struggle through this rehearsal, somehow convince Craig not to come to opening night, and find some sort of excuse for my brilliant understudy—Annabelle, that is—to take over the part. And I would have to warn my friends to be careful never to bring up this play in front of Craig again. Then I could move on to figuring out how to work my way around some of my other lies—about my parents, about dating other guys. And even if I managed all that, I still wouldn't be finished. I'd have to maintain the lies whenever Craig and I were together, never letting myself completely relax, never letting him know the real me, honestly and completely. . . .

Annabelle poked me. "Heads up," she murmured. "Don't get distracted, or you'll miss your next cue."

I had reached a decision. And I couldn't wait for my cue. If I hesitated for even a second, I knew I would probably chicken out. My whole body was already shaking at the thought of what I was about to do.

I strode onto the stage immediately, ignoring Annabelle's attempts to stop me. Heading straight past the other actors, I stepped to the edge.

"Excuse me," I said. My voice came out in a squeak, all but drowned out by the orchestra. I cleared my throat and tried again. "Excuse me!"

This time I projected well enough to make Mr. Dinsdale proud—although pride wasn't the expression on his face just at that moment. He was staring up at me in utter confusion. So was Craig, but I did my best to ignore that.

I waved my hands around and continued to yell, "Excuse me" until the orchestra wound down into a series of tentative toots and trills, then finally fell silent.

"Thank you," I said. My pulse was pounding through every artery. I forced myself to go on. "I'm sorry, everyone," I said. "Thanks for letting me step in tonight, but I don't think this is working. I'm going to let Annabelle take over, okay?"

Mr. Dinsdale gave me a long, penetrating look.

Then he jumped up onstage beside me and clapped his hands.

"Okay, folks," he called. "Let's take ten to regroup and let Annabelle get ready. Then we'll try it again from the top."

In the flurry of activity that followed, I didn't have time to see Craig's response. I'd been afraid to even glance at him while I was speaking, and as soon as Mr. Dinsdale made his announcement the orchestra members all jumped to their feet, blocking my view of the first row. Before I could make a move, Mr. Dinsdale hustled me backstage to the dressing room.

Annabelle was waiting for me there. "What was that all about?" she asked as she quickly helped me unzip my dress.

"I have no idea." I felt like a robot. I wasn't thinking anything much. I was just waiting. Waiting for the moment I would have to face Craig and explain myself. Then I'd be thinking and feeling plenty. "I think—I think I just decided to be honest with Craig."

Annabelle took a step back and stared at me. "Who are you, and what have you done with Jill?" she demanded.

"I'm serious," I protested. I watched as she started to remove the pins from Eliza's dress. The thoughts and feelings were already starting to seep back. "Um, listen. Break a leg, okay? I'll see you later."

"Okay." Annabelle smiled at me. "You break a leg too, okay?"

*　　　*　　　*

I didn't let Craig say a word until we were outside, well away from the theater, in a little spot of parkland on the shores of the lake.

Then I turned to him. In the light of the streetlight a few yards away, his handsome face looked totally perplexed. I took a deep breath. I'd never been so scared in my entire life. It was positively paralyzing. I could no longer feel my body—just my mind, throbbing with what I was about to say. So much was at risk. For a second I thought I wasn't going to be able to go through with it.

But I hadn't left myself much choice. And more important, I knew I really had changed in the past few days. I wouldn't be able to live with myself if I didn't do this.

"Craig." My voice only shook a little. "I have something important to tell you."

Sixteen

Craig

I HAD NO idea what was going on. First Jill had
called a halt to her dress rehearsal. Then she'd
dragged me halfway across town, refusing to say a
word or to let me say anything. Now we were
standing in some kind of lakeside park, and I was
about as confused as I'd ever been in my life. Were
actresses always unpredictable like this?

I stared down at her. Her face looked pale and
her eyes were dark.

"What's going on?" I asked, trying very hard
not to sound annoyed. As I may have mentioned, I
don't like being confused. I don't like it at all.

Jill held up a hand to silence me before I could
say anything more. "Let me explain," she said
softly. "It's not going to be easy for me, and I don't
know how you're going to react. But please, just
promise you'll let me get it all out before you say
anything, okay?"

That sounded rather ominous, but I just nodded. Whatever she had to say, how bad could it be?

She took a deep breath. "Craig, I've been lying to you."

That got my attention. Big time. But I just looked at her and waited for her to go on, not letting myself react until I heard more.

"I'm not in that play. I never was," she went on in a rush of words. "My friend Annabelle is the one who's really playing Eliza Doolittle. I—I just told you I had play rehearsals all those times because . . . um, because I was going out with other guys and I didn't want you to know."

A rush of white-hot anger hit me. I could hardly believe it. She'd been deceiving me all along. Playing games. Playing the field. Ed had tried to warn me.

"There's more." Her voice was shaking now. I guessed she'd read the expression on my face. "There was no anniversary party for my parents. Actually, my parents are divorced. That was another cover-up. So was that stupid jellyfish story. When you saw me in the car with Romeo, I'd just come from a date with another guy."

I felt completely betrayed. It hurt like nothing I'd ever felt. I gulped, trying to maintain control. All my earlier happy thoughts and plans came crashing down around me. How could I have been so gullible? So much for an honest relationship.

She was searching my face. "I just knew we couldn't have a real relationship if you didn't know

166

the truth. About the other guys and—and everything."

"How many other guys are we talking about here?" I asked. The pain bewildered me, making me want to curl up into a ball and stay there. How could I be hurt so badly by a girl I'd met just a couple of weeks before? It wasn't fair.

"Not that many," she said quickly. Then she gulped. "Well, actually, I shouldn't say that. You might think it was kind of a lot, I guess."

"How many?" I asked again. "I know about the guy at the pizza place. Who else are we talking about? Anybody I know? My brother, perhaps?" I added bitterly.

Jill's eyes were looking a little watery, but I forced myself not to be affected. I had to shut down the part of me that had fallen for her. Or for whoever she'd led me to believe she was.

She shook her head. "You don't know any of them," she said. "It doesn't matter. I don't care about them. I only care about you."

That last line came out almost in a whisper. I pushed it aside in my mind. "I want to know, Jill," I said, my voice steely. "I *deserve* to know."

She bit her lip. For a second I didn't think she was going to answer. Then she did. She gave me the list. It seemed to go on forever. Each new name was like a stab in the heart. A stab with a sharp, splintery stake coated in Tabasco sauce.

How could she have done it? How could she have lied to me, betrayed me? My face burned as I thought of that guy I'd chatted with back at the theater, Roger. Had she told him about me? And how could she have gone out with that lame singer in that loser band? Had she kissed him? Had she kissed all of them the way she'd kissed me?

Jill was waiting for a response, but I didn't know what to say. This was all happening way too fast. What had made me think that Jill and I were ready for a real relationship after knowing each other for less than two weeks? What had made me think we were right for each other at all?

"Craig?" Jill asked tentatively. "I don't blame you for being upset. All I can say is, I'm sorry. I really don't care about any of those other guys. I never did. Just like you don't care about that other girl. You're the first guy I've ever been serious about. It just took me a while to realize it."

I was going to have to speak sooner or later, I knew that. But I still had no idea what to say.

The longer I stayed silent, the more upset she looked. Before long tears started trickling down her face. I couldn't help noticing that she looked beautiful even when she cried.

But that didn't matter anymore, did it? For all I knew, her tears were fake too.

"Craig," she sobbed, "I didn't know what else to do. I'm sorry. I'm really, really sorry. Can't we talk about this? Is there any chance we can work it out?"

"I don't know, Jill," I said carefully. "I really don't know. I need some time to figure it out."

Then I turned and walked away, leaving her standing there alone.

The next evening I sat on the edge of my bed and stared at the ticket in my hand. It was for the opening night of *My Fair Lady*. It had been waiting for me in a plain white envelope marked with my name when I'd arrived at work at the candy store that morning. As soon as I'd opened the envelope and seen what it was, that jabbing pain had shot through my heart again, replacing the dull throbbing ache that had settled there sometime the night before.

Jill. She'd left it for me, of course. She wanted to work things out. Did I?

I remembered how I'd felt when I'd first spotted her in that crowded pizza place. I remembered her laughter and the feel of her hand on my arm as we strolled through the darkened streets. And I remembered how she'd looked as she rushed across the street to meet me at the movies, breathless and flushed . . .

From her date with another guy, a small voice reminded me cruelly.

I didn't know what to do. It had kept me up all night, distracted me all day. She claimed she cared about me. But she'd lied before. Was she telling the truth now? Could she really change her ways? And could I afford to take a chance that might bring me even more pain and heartbreak? Was she worth it?

★   ★   ★

I arrived at the theater a few minutes before show time. It looked totally different than it had the night before. The lights were dim and the lobby was filled with excited, chattering people.

I saw a couple of waiters come out of the theater with trays full of empty dishes and deduced that I'd missed the dinner part of the dinner theater experience. I wasn't too upset about that. I couldn't have eaten just at that moment for anything. My stomach was a hard, shriveled knot.

An usher was waiting just inside the wide double doors. He pointed me toward a tiny round table near the back of the room.

She was there already. Her back was to me. This was my last chance to turn back.

But I couldn't.

I cleared my throat as I reached the table and she turned immediately. Her eyes, huge quivering pools, drew my gaze like a magnet.

She opened her mouth to speak, but nothing came out at first except a small squeak. She cleared her throat and tried again. "Hello, Craig," she said.

I pulled out my chair and sat down. Once I managed to get past her eyes, I noticed that the rest of her looked absolutely stunning—she was wearing a silky blue dress that clung softly to her curves and set off her sea-colored eyes. "Hi," I said. "I thought we should talk."

She nodded but didn't say anything. She was waiting for me to start.

And suddenly my mind was a blank. I had no idea what I wanted to say. What I wanted to happen next.

Before I figured it out, the lights flickered a few times, then dimmed. The orchestra members picked up their instruments. The show was starting.

Seventeen

Jill

I MUST HAVE breathed during the first act of the show, but I couldn't swear to it. I felt as though everything had stopped: my heart, my lungs, my circulation. My entire body felt numb and cold.

The sight of Craig walking into the theater had felt the way a sip of water must feel to a person dying of thirst. But once that sip is over, then what? If there's a whole bucket of water behind it, great. But if that sip is all you get, maybe it just prolongs the pain.

Had I done the right thing by telling him? I had lain awake all night wondering. Maybe I shouldn't have been quite so honest about how many guys I'd gone out with. Maybe I should have confessed to one or two dates and left it at that.

But what would have been the point? This thing with Craig was different from anything I'd known before. I wouldn't have been able to go on deceiving him. I couldn't have done it and still looked into that honest, handsome, totally wonderful face. The face that had looked so cold just now . . .

Had he shown up just to tell me it was over? Most guys wouldn't bother. Then again, most guys weren't Craig. Maybe he was so decent and responsible that he wouldn't feel right just walking away from whatever it was we'd almost had. Maybe he felt compelled to say good-bye like an adult. I just hoped I could handle it. Either way, I was glad I'd decided to drop off that ticket. At least it would be settled that night, one way or the other. Not knowing was pure agony.

I stared sightlessly at the stage. Annabelle seemed to be wowing the audience. There was loud, enthusiastic applause after every scene and every song. But I wasn't aware of a single note.

Now that I knew what it was like to care about someone, *really* care, I could never go back to my old ways. And if Craig didn't want me, I didn't know what I'd do. Become a nun, maybe.

This was just too hard. What was Craig thinking as he sat beside me in the dark?

It seemed for a while that intermission would never come. But when it did, it took me by surprise. I wasn't ready. I couldn't face this.

As the lights came up I turned toward Craig. His face already seemed so familiar to me. Those deep, serious eyes. That thick hair. The strong line of his nose. I drank in the sight of him, trying to memorize every inch. I couldn't read his expression. He didn't look angry, exactly. But he didn't look happy either.

The waiters were already bustling toward us. Dinner had been served earlier, but I hadn't been able to eat a bite—I'd been too sick at the realization that he wasn't going to show. But dessert always came at intermission. So Craig and I were forced to keep silent for a few more endless, excruciating minutes.

Finally the waiters were gone. I turned to look at him again, hardly able to bear the tension. If he didn't speak soon, I was going to explode into shards of pure hysteria.

He stared back. His green eyes shimmered with an emotion I couldn't pinpoint.

Then he did the last thing I ever would have expected.

He leaned over the table—and kissed me!

For a second I was too stunned even to kiss him back. Then I couldn't help it. I reached over and grabbed him by the shoulders, giving it all I had. If this was his way of saying good-bye, I was going to make it count!

Finally he pulled away. "It's just as I thought," he said.

"What?" I murmured, feeling slightly light-headed from the kiss.

He smiled. "There's no way I can give that up," he said. "I don't care about all those other guys." He paused. "Well, maybe I do care. A little. But I'll get over it. I have to. I can't change the past, and neither can you."

I was starting to get the gist of what he was saying. It was almost too good to be true. Did I dare to believe it? "But we *can* control the future," I said softly, believing it with all my heart. "Especially if we do it together."

"Right." He reached for my hand and squeezed it tightly. "I've never felt like this about anyone. It's kind of scary. There's so much at stake if it doesn't work out. But I'm willing to take the risk. It's worth it to me. *You're* worth it to me."

I smiled. "I sure am glad to hear that." All the tension of the past few days melted away, and I felt like laughing out loud, dancing on the table, and shrieking for sheer joy. Naturally, I held myself back, settling for a huge grin instead. This night wasn't the end I had feared. It was the beginning of something I hadn't even realized I wanted until it hit me over the head.

I wouldn't change the past if I could. No way. Because the past had led me—led *us*—to this moment in the present. And the present was shaping up to be very, very interesting. Not to mention the future . . .

I had so much more to say to him. But there was all the time in the world to do it now. And words just didn't seem to be enough at this moment. So instead, I pulled him toward me and kissed him again.

This time neither of us pulled away, even when the curtain went up for the second act. Somehow I was pretty sure that Annabelle wouldn't mind.

Do you ever wonder about falling in love? About members of the opposite sex? Do you need a little friendly advice but have no one to turn to? Well, that's where we come in . . . Jenny and Jake. Send us those questions you're dying to ask, and we'll give you the straight scoop on life and love in the nineties.

DEAR JAKE

Q: *I have a boyfriend, Pete, and we've been together for four months. The problem is that I kind of have a crush on this other guy, Joe. I don't know if Joe likes me, though, so I don't want to ruin what I have with Pete only to be rejected by Joe. Plus, I still want to at least be friends with Pete, and I'm afraid he won't want to be if I leave him for another guy. What should I do?*

ML, Eudora, KS

A: First of all, I don't think you and Pete have much of a relationship if you're thinking about other guys. Whether or not you end up with Joe, it's time to be straight with Pete about your feelings. No matter what, it's not going to be easy for him to accept that the girl he's totally into just wants to be a buddy, but if you handle the situation with sensitivity, you might be able to salvage a friendship.

As for Joe, wait to pursue him until things are settled with Pete. Otherwise, both guys might feel like you're playing games. Once you're a free agent, let Joe know that you're interested and leave the ball in his court.

Q: *I like this guy, Tom, but he's really shy, so I'm not sure how he feels about me. I have no problem making the first move if I have to, but I'm a little worried that maybe he's turned off by aggressive girls. Should I go ahead and ask him out, or should I wait for him to do something?*

JY, Memphis, TN

A: Just because a guy is shy doesn't mean that he wants girls to be equally timid. If Tom is interested in you but can't work up the nerve to let you know, he'll probably be relieved and thrilled when you take the initiative. There are a few guys left who believe in the old-school tradition that guys should do the asking, but this is increasingly rare. We love it when the burden isn't completely on us, and it sure gives our egos a good boost to have a pretty girl come along and flirt a little.

However, if Tom is shy, the whole moment might be awkward and overwhelming for him. Try not to make a big deal out of the whole thing; be casual and friendly and the experience will be painless for both of you!

Q: *I met Ralph almost a year ago, and it seemed like we were really hitting it off. Then he moved away, and he never answered my letters or returned my phone calls. A few weeks ago he moved back to my neighborhood. He wants to go out with me, but I don't know if I can trust him, since last time he left he totally forgot about me. Do I give him another chance?*

CF, Westerville, OH

A: This is a tricky one. It's possible that his intentions were good, and then once he moved he just got caught up in his new life and kept *meaning* to send a letter or pick up the phone, but other things came up. I know, I know—why is it so hard for us guys to take five minutes and call you? Well, maybe leaving you was traumatic for Ralph, and he figured it would be easier to deal with it if he didn't have to be reminded of what he was missing out on. Yeah, it's pretty wimpy, but if it's true, then at least his heart is in the right place.

On the other hand, he could be a player who assumes that you've been waiting around for him. Maybe he just wants to be with you when it's convenient for him. Ouch, that hurts—but if it's true, you need to know so that you can protect yourself. What it comes down to is that you'll need to trust your instincts about Ralph; make him work a little to prove he's for real, and if he sticks it out and you still want to be with him, go for it.

DEAR JENNY

Q: *When I was fifteen, my boyfriend Sam was killed in a car accident. We'd only been together for a few months, but I knew that he was the one and I was devastated. That was a year ago, and I still think about him all the time and I miss him so much. But recently I met this really sweet, funny guy and he actually makes me feel happy in a way I haven't since Sam died. He asked me out, but I wasn't sure if I should say yes. Is it still too soon to fall in love with someone else?*

JA, Davie, FL

A: Mourning a loved one is a long and difficult process. Losing Sam was extra hard because you were both so young and you had such a short time together. It's natural that you would still think about him a lot and that you would feel guilty about letting yourself love anyone else. But you *are* still young, and your life didn't end when Sam's did. He would want you to be happy, and if this new guy helps that happen, then it's definitely a good idea to go out with him. Just feel free to move slowly, and let the guy know that it will take time for you to feel comfortable being with him, since your last relationship ended so tragically.

Q: *Okay, I am so awful and I know it, but I don't know what to do. Jacob and I get along really well, we have tons in common, and he's a sweetheart. He wants us to be more than friends, and I should want that too but I'm just not attracted to him! Is there any way to get past that, or do I just have to be a terrible human being and turn the guy down because I can't imagine kissing him?*

LM, Salisbury, MD

A: You are *not* a terrible human being just because your pulse doesn't race when Jacob is near you. We can't pick and choose who we have chemistry with and who we don't; sometimes it just isn't there no matter how badly you wish it were. Of course, there are times when you don't *think* you're attracted to someone and then once you let yourself have a romantic evening alone, you suddenly realize that his eyes are actually more green than brown and that smile of his is pretty cute. If you think there's a chance your feelings could change and you genuinely want a romantic relationship with Jacob, give it a try. But it's possible that your lack of desire comes from the fact that he'll never be more than a good friend, and if that's the case, you'll have to find a way to let him down gently.

Q: *I've liked Scott for a while, and we've even kissed a few times, but he's never really up for a commitment. Now his friend Ricky says he likes me. Ricky's cute and all, and he's a nice guy, but I'm pretty hung up on Scott. However, ever since Ricky said he liked me, Scott has been acting more interested. I'm so confused; I don't know if I should go out with Ricky, since he treats me well, or wait for Scott to figure out how perfect we are for each other.*

AM, Houston, TX

A: Do not date Ricky just to make Scott jealous, or just because you feel like you should. If you're not interested, leave it at a friendship. If you lead him on when you know it's not right, Ricky will just get hurt worse in the end.

I'm sure you already knew I'd warn you about this, but I have to say it anyway: Scott might only be pursuing you now because he wants to show up his friend, prove that he's got more power. Maybe it really took seeing another guy go after you to make him realize his true feelings, but no matter what, he's not being a good friend to Ricky. If you don't care about any of this and want him anyway, it's time to confront him and make him decide one way or the other where things stand between you.

Do you have questions about love? Write to:
Jenny Burgess or Jake Korman
c/o Daniel Weiss Associates
33 West 17th Street
New York, NY 10011

Don't miss any of the books in *Love Stories*
—the romantic series from Bantam Books!

#1 *My First Love* . . . . Callie West

#2 *Sharing Sam* . . . . Katherine Applegate

#3 *How to Kiss a Guy* . . . . Elizabeth Bernard

#4 *The Boy Next Door* . . . . Janet Quin-Harkin

#5 *The Day I Met Him* . . . . Catherine Clark

#6 *Love Changes Everything* . . . . . . ArLynn Presser

#7 *More Than a Friend* . . . . Elizabeth Winfrey

#8 *The Language of Love* . . . . Kate Emburg

#9 *My So-called Boyfriend* . . . . . . Elizabeth Winfrey

#10 *It Had to Be You* . . . . Stephanie Doyon

#11 *Some Girls Do* . . . . Dahlia Kosinski

#12 *Hot Summer Nights* . . . . Elizabeth Chandler

#13 *Who Do You Love?* . . . . Janet Quin-Harkin

#14 *Three-Guy Weekend* . . . . Alexis Page

#15 *Never Tell Ben* . . . . Diane Namm

#16 *Together Forever* . . . . Cameron Dokey

#17 *Up All Night* . . . . Karen Michaels

#18 *24/7* . . . . Amy S. Wilensky

#19 *It's a Prom Thing* . . . . Diane Schwemm

#20 *The Guy I Left Behind* . . . . Ali Brooke

#21 *He's Not What You Think* . . . . . Randi Reisfeld

#22 *A Kiss Between Friends* . . . . Erin Haft

#23 *The Rumor About Julia* . . . . . . Stephanie Sinclair

#24 *Don't Say Good-bye* . . . . Diane Schwemm

#25 *Crushing on You* . . . . Wendy Loggia

#26 *Our Secret Love* . . . . Miranda Harry

#27 *Trust Me* . . . . Kieran Scott

#28 *He's the One* . . . . Nina Alexander

Super Editions

Listen to My Heart . . . . Katherine Applegate
Kissing Caroline . . . . Cheryl Zach
It's Different for Guys . . . . Stephanie Leighton
My Best Friend's Girlfriend . . . . Wendy Loggia
Love Happens . . . . Elizabeth Chandler
Out of My League . . . . Everett Owens

Coming soon:

#29 Kiss and Tell . . . . Kieran Scott

Real *life.*
Real *friends.*
Real *faith.*

Introducing Clearwater Crossing—

where friendships are formed, hearts
come together, choices have consequences,
and lives are changed forever...

Even friends have secrets.

Reality

laura peyton roberts

#2   0-553-57121-4

Friends ... but for how long?

Get a Life

laura peyton roberts

#1   0-553-57118-4

clearwater crossing

An inspirational new series available March 9, 1998,
wherever books are sold.

Watch out
Sweet Valley
University—
the Wakefield
twins are
on campus!

Jessica and Elizabeth are away
at college, with no parental
supervision! Going to classes
and parties . . . learning about
careers and college guys . . .
they're having the time of their
lives. Join your favorite twins as
they become SVU's favorite coeds!